"Yes, I'm questioning your ability."

Karl said the words matter-of-factly, and Paula looked at him in wide-eyed astonishment.

"Then find someone else for the job." Paula squared her shoulders before continuing. "Because I don't think I'm prepared—"

"Prepared—or qualified?" Karl interrupted her.

"You know what I'm going to do?" she asked. "I'm going to throw you out of here. I'm not prepared to consider working for you. What's really bothering you is the fact that this business is owned, and run, by a woman."

Wynne May was born near Johannesburg, South Africa. Shortly after graduating from college, she began working for the South African Broadcasting Corporation. While on holiday, she met Claude, the handsome green-eyed stranger who spoke to her after she slipped and fell into a swimming pool! Three months later Claude slipped a diamond ring on to Wynne's finger as they stood under the stars in an exotic garden. Wynne now spends her time with her family—and writing romances.

DESERT ROSE
Wynne May

Harlequin Books

TORONTO • NEW YORK • LONDON
AMSTERDAM • PARIS • SYDNEY • HAMBURG
STOCKHOLM • ATHENS • TOKYO • MILAN
MADRID • WARSAW • BUDAPEST • AUCKLAND

ISBN 0-373-17188-9

DESERT ROSE

Copyright © 1993 by Wynne May.

This edition published by arrangement with Harlequin Enterprises B. V.

® and TM are trademarks of the publisher. Trademarks indicated with
® are registered in the United States Patent and Trademark Office, the
Canadian Trade Marks Office and in other countries.

Printed in U.S.A.

CHAPTER ONE

To REACH Agate Beach and Sturmvögel, and the castle situated there, Paula Stewart had driven eight kilometres from Lüderitz, a small town built on the rugged and bare rocks of that large, continuous and restless mass of land known as Africa.

Situated between the merciless Namib Desert, diamond dunes and sea, Lüderitz and its monotonous coastline could have been at the end of the earth, she thought.

The austere sandstone fortification had been built as a home for a German immigrant, Count Horst von Buren, in 1909. Another German, a baron, so the story went, had also commenced building an imposing *schloss* near by. A number of the baron's artisans had ended up by being employed by Horst von Buren — one of them being Paula's great-grandfather, Rory Paul Stewart, who was a carpenter.

Leaving a young wife and two sons, Rory Stewart had followed the advice of a friend who was already in South-West Africa, and had come from Ireland in the hopes of finding work as a carpenter and, eventually, of sending for his little family. After eighteen months, during which time he had faithfully written to his wife, he had disappeared and was never heard of again.

Since Paula intended writing a book based on her great-grandmother's extensive diaries and her great-grandfather's letters, she had come out to what was now Namibia, not only to research her background but also in the hopes of finding out what had happened to Rory Paul Stewart all those years ago. After all, she reasoned, tales of the past had always been handed down from one generation to another.

So far she had been unsuccessful and was more than ready to go back home, but, since she had found herself short of money, she had had no option but to stay on in Lüderitz. Her father had recently experienced the trauma of going insolvent and she could hardly write to him for financial assistance.

Situated as it was on one of the best natural harbours along the Atlantic coastline and with an important fishing industry and nearby diamond diggings to add to its good fortune, Lüderitz had once been an active port. It had experienced a boom in the early years of the century when diamonds were found, but the mines had long since been abandoned and the population of the town had dwindled. Recently, however, visitors seemed to be finding the atmosphere of Lüderitz appealing and, what was more important, remote from the pressures of everyday life. People kept returning, and for this reason a number of cottages had been — and still were being — repaired and restored as holiday homes.

With a degree in architecture and a little experience behind her, Paula had been prompted to start a small business which she called Odd Jobbers, and up to the present time, she and her two handymen had not found it too difficult to obtain work. As a result, her impoverished bank balance was beginning to show an improvement.

Getting out of the second-hand pick-up she had bought in the interest of this business, she made her way towards the outside steps leading up to the deserted castle which stood on a rocky rise above the long and curved stretch of beach.

The heavy door, with its coat of arms set in stone above it, seemed to mock her as usual, as she stood there, unable to get in. The door showed signs of having been battered by fierce gales which had blown in from the Atlantic and from being attacked by flying particles of sand.

The latest news, passed on to Paula by Herr Heinrich Wolff who managed a curio shop and lived in a cottage near to her own, was that the Castle Sturmvögel was going to be restored, after which, since tourism was on the upswing, it was going to be opened to the public.

Turning to gaze at the beach, the sea and the many seabirds, she found herself thinking that some of the growth clinging to the wavy sand resembled clumps of matted hair. Many of these clusters were even adorned with what appeared to be green ribbon.

When she spotted a Land Rover, heading in the direction of the castle, she swore softly.

The man who got out of the Land Rover a few moments later was dark-haired and was wearing blue jeans and a dark blue T-shirt, and even from where she was standing Paula found she couldn't take her eyes off him.

When he reached her, he took off his sunglasses, and she immediately noticed his assessing steel-grey look which travelled quickly from her auburn hair to the striped trousers in stone and white, which she was wearing with a dusky pink shirt, then back to her face.

Returning this unnerving steel-grey gaze, she felt as if some potent narcotic was going to work on her and inducing hypnosis.

'This comes as a surprise.' His accent was attractive, and when he smiled, two lines on either side of his mouth deepened. 'I hardly expected to find company out here.' He ran his fingers through his straight glossy hair and then swept it back from his forehead. As she watched him, Paula was struck again by the sheer physical magnetism of him.

'Why *are* you here?' he asked bluntly.

'Is there any reason why I shouldn't be?' she asked.

He laughed. 'No, of course not! I'm just curious.'

She could imagine this man soaking up the sun in a Mediterranean playground, or enjoying the snow at some ski-resort—the sparkling, frosted countryside of fashionable Gstaad, maybe, or St Moritz, where the rich met to enjoy winter sports. . . Wherever he was, there was bound to be a stunning girl in the picture.

'I was just about to leave.' Paula found her eyes straying to his mouth. 'It's getting late, and that road leaves a lot to be desired.'

He smiled and glanced at his watch. 'It's not as late as all that, so please don't leave on my account. You haven't told me why you're here, and after all, it's a lonely spot and, as you say, the road leaves a lot to be desired.'

'You'd get a shock if I told you.'

His grey eyes narrowed slightly. 'Oh? Why is that?'

Paula laughed lightly. 'I was contemplating breaking in, actually.'

'*What?*' He had an infectious laugh, she thought. 'In that case, we shall have to have you arrested, no? But in any event I think you'd have a difficult task ahead of you.'

After a slight pause she said, 'Tell me, are you who I think you are?'

He seemed amused. 'And who do you think I am?'

'Well——' she felt a sudden sense of exhilaration '—*news* has it that Sturmvögel is to be restored shortly, after which it's going to be opened to the public. *News* also has it that someone would be coming out from Germany to get things going — so you must be that someone.'

'Like the bird-life in these parts, news travels quickly, no?' He gave her a disarming smile. 'I am Karl von Buren. Horst, my great-grandfather, built this place.'

'Oh, no!' Paula went on looking at him. 'I just don't believe it! So you're actually a von Buren? *My* great-grandfather, Rory Paul Stewart, worked here as a carpenter. He came out from Ireland. If you only knew how I've been *longing* to get into this place!'

'Really? And you are?' he queried.

'I'm Paula Stewart, named after *him* — Rory Paul. Don't ask me why.'

'And so, Paula, you have come all the way from Ireland, I take it, just to see where this great-grandfather of yours worked?' His gaze was thoughtful and lingering.

'As a matter of fact,' she told him, 'I came out to research the background of a book I intend writing, which will be based on my great-grandmother's diaries and the letters which Rory wrote to her. He never returned to Ireland. What happened to him has remained a complete mystery. He just disappeared off the face of the earth and nobody heard another thing — certainly not his wife, who was left with two young sons. I've been hoping to find out something while I'm here.'

'It would appear that you are as spirited as your great-grandfather.' Once again his grey eyes travelled the length of her. 'Well, if this old castle could talk it would have countless tales to tell, by the sound of it. Unfortunately, it cannot talk, but maybe on the other hand that is fortunate. Who knows?'

Paula felt prompted to go on with her story. 'I keep wondering whether he could have disappeared while on a long walk or something. For instance, on the way to what's known as Dias Point, there's a grave with the words "George Pond of London died here of hunger and thirst 1906" on the cross. The same thing could have happened to Rory, I suppose. Or maybe he found his way to the Skeleton Coast, which is fog-bound and very desolate, not to mention very treacherous, and got lost. To get back to George Pond, though, for some reason or another, he was actually run out of Lüderitz without food or water, which was a terrible thing to have happened. The poor man tried to shelter on one of the islands — but my point is, it just goes to show what could — and still can — happen when one finds oneself without food or water in the desert.'

Karl von Buren seemed genuinely interested. 'Why would he have gone to the Skeleton Coast? Is that not the area where many ships were wrecked? Would it have been possible that he had gone there to search for treasure?'

'He might have gone to look for *diamonds*! Apart from the wrecked ships along the coastline, skeletons have been found of Portuguese wanderers — probably after the same thing. Pistols have also been found — even a pouch of gold coins. I'm being morbid, aren't I?' Paula smiled. 'But these are all dreadful reminders of what happened to adventuresome people all those years ago.'

'It is a pity I had not known you were here — *and* longing to break into the castle!' The fascinating lines on either side of his mouth deepened, as he smiled. 'As it happens, there have been keys here in Lüderitz for years. They were left with Heinrich Wolff — you may even know him — by my father when he was out here a number of years ago. I could have arranged for you to have the keys and you could have come here whenever you wished.'

'The keys have been with Herr Heinrich? Everybody calls him that, by the way.' Paula's voice contained all the surprise she felt at hearing this.

The old blighter! she was thinking. How typical of Heinrich who, with his mild manner and white moustache, was known to the locals as a deep one. Since he had known of her frustration at not being able to see the interior of the castle, where her great-grandfather had worked for eighteen months before disappearing, surely he might have at least told her?

'And so you intend writing a book?' Karl von Buren broke into her thoughts.

'Yes. All the letters he wrote from here described the conditions, which I've now mostly seen for myself, of course. He described everything—how, for instance, material from Germany arrived via Lüderitz and was transported, along with stone from some quarry, by ox-wagons.'

'I am more than just a little interested to hear all this,' Karl told her. 'You see, my mother is also in possession of the diaries of Horst and Hannah, his wife. I really must try to find out more about this in an endeavour to be of help to you. One thing does stand out in my mind, though. . .when the castle was completed he wrote, "We shared the satisfaction of a job well done. Throughout, our enthusiasm—and that goes for everybody—knew no bounds." Something like that, anyway.'

'Well, it *was* a feat, after all.' Paula gazed up at the sandstone fortress. 'To them it must have been like building their own pyramid, don't you think?'

He laughed. 'I guess you could say that. Tell me, how long will you be here?'

Paula was aware, again, of his long, assessing look, and suddenly she was pleased that her financial difficulties had kept her here.

'Oh, for some time yet. I'm renting a little cottage in Lüderitz. And you? When did you arrive?'

'Two days ago, from Windhoek, where I had been for a few days.' He turned to look at the Land

Rover. 'I bought the Land Rover in Windhoek and drove to the desert-besieged port of Lüderitz,' his tone was slightly mocking, 'and on to here. While the necessary repairs are taking place and up until the time Sturmvögel has been sold, I will be living here — God help me!' He laughed softly. 'Anyway, without having to resort to breaking in, allow me to invite you into the castle which has caused you so much frustration.'

A sudden uneasiness spread through Paula. One moment she had been longing for just this to happen and the next she found herself wondering whether she would be doing the right thing by accepting his offer. After all, no matter how exciting he was, or how handsome, or what the connection was with Herr Heinrich, to her Karl von Buren was a perfect stranger.

As he began to unlock the massive door, he seemed to sense her thoughts. Without turning he said, 'Do I *look* dangerous?' His tone was mocking.

'Actually, I *was* thinking along those lines — yes, you look highly dangerous, since your looks *are* rather picaresque,' she told him.

He laughed softly. 'I am not dangerous, neither am I a rogue, but that is for you to find out, no? What had you in mind?' He turned to look at her. 'That since I find your unusual turquoise-blue eyes and scarlet hair tantalising, I might lock you in a secret chamber, which exists here, and have my way with you?'

Paula felt the colour which had begun to tint her cheeks. '*Scarlet* hair?' She tried to sound amused. 'Anyway, you'll have me running away in a moment!'

He stood to one side for her to enter the big hall. 'This room is known as a *Rittersaal*, by the way. In other words—the big hall.'

'Well, it certainly answers to the name.' She glanced around. 'By the way, I should have mentioned. . .I can't stay all that long. I have that road to think of, and there could always be a sandstorm. They mostly occur in the afternoons—especially just out of Lüderitz—but here anything is possible.'

'I experienced a sandstorm on the way here from Windhoek,' he told her. 'Please overlook the disorder everywhere. I haven't yet had time to sort myself out.'

The next room he showed her into was obviously intended as the main sitting-room, and there was a huge fireplace at one end.

'But I'm *amazed* to find it furnished—and I don't see the disorder. I've heard, of course, that the castle changed hands many times, complete with most of its contents, but somehow I never imagined that there was furniture behind those walls.'

Paula watched him as he went towards a console table where there was an array of bottles, decanters and glasses, which he must have looked out from somewhere.

'Most of the furniture has remained here. Strangely enough, Sturmvögel *has* always, as you say, been sold with most of its contents, and at one particular time in history, it had been bought for the purpose of providing tourist accommodation. It was then, I understand, decided to remove everything while alterations were going on. Although this did in fact take place, these alterations did not, and there was, after all, to be no accommodation for tourists. The furniture came back. Most of it belonged to Horst von Buren. Strangely enough, it was only while the castle was empty — that is, when the furniture and important works of art, glass and chinaware had been removed — that a certain amount of vandalism occurred. This has resulted in the inevitable backlog of repairs, which you'll soon see for yourself. It is going to be my lot in life to get these repairs and alterations under way.'

He had uncorked a bottle of white wine and he began to pour the wine into heirloom-looking glasses.

'In Windhoek I made sure I'd make myself comfortable here, believe me, since I did not know what I would find here,' he went on. 'I went on a massive shopping spree, buying things like boldly coloured sheets — to cheer the lonely nights — towels, soap and even foodstuffs which would, of course, not perish on the way here. And then I was able in Lüderitz yesterday to buy ice and two more polystyrene cool-bags. You see, there is no refrigerator here. Until I get the generator working, there is no electricity, for that matter. I might even have to buy a new generator, for all I know.'

'How come Sturmvögel has changed hands so often,' Paula asked, 'only to land back as the property of the von Buren family?'

He shrugged. 'It's a long story. Horst, for reasons he thought best, sold it and then my grandfather bought it back one day — only to sell it again, at a later stage. Then, in turn, my father wanted it back in the family. You must realise, of course, that wars played a big part here. It is a well-known fact that wars uproot people and rip families apart. The average man does not plan it that way, it's just the way it seems to turn out, no?'

He came over to Paula and handed her a glass of wine, and as she took it she said, 'You mentioned vandalism just now. Let me put it on record,' she laughed lightly, 'since I was unable to break in — or was even around until fairly recently, in fact — I'm not guilty.'

'I'll take your word for it,' he teased. 'I don't think you'd have the strength, anyway.'

Thinking of the kind of work she did, she laughed. 'Don't you? You'd be surprised!'

'Let's drink our wine as we look around,' he suggested. 'You will notice that most of the rooms are panelled and beamed, and in view of the fact that your great-grandfather was probably behind most of it, if not all of it, this should interest you.'

After they had been through several interesting rooms Paula glanced at her watch. 'Well, I do have to get back to Lüderitz, so I'd better say thank-you and be on my way.'

'Come here whenever you wish.' There seemed to be a challenge in the words. 'Come and write here. Feel free.'

'Thank you.' As she looked into his eyes, she felt their steel-grey magnetism. 'You know, this is an act of fate — you turning up here in Lüderitz just at the right time for me.'

'And so you believe in fate?' He smiled easily, while his slightly narrowed eyes held hers.

'Let's just say I don't underestimate it — but yes, I suppose I do. Don't you?'

'At this moment, yes.' As he spoke, she was suddenly aware of the sexual interest between them.

As casually as she could she went on, 'You would wonder why on earth your great-grand-father built here, wouldn't you? And above all things, a castle. Windhoek I could understand. After all, there are about three or four castles there, but here — on this wild stretch of beach?'

'Maybe it was just that — the rocks, sea, sand and desert. Maybe that's what he wanted — but there is, I must admit, something alien about the whole set-up. By building a castle he probably thought his family would be safer here. I guess he also wanted to capture some of the rich heritage of his family's past. To me, of course, it is baffling to see a desert on the edge of the sea and virtually at my back door.'

Paula found herself laughing. 'It sounds so funny to hear you referring to the back door of a castle! I suppose, through his diaries, you would have learned quite a bit about him?'

Karl thought for a moment. '*Ja*. . .well, Horst was tall, dark-haired and handsome, and leaned, I believe, on an elegant walking stick which was topped by a rose-quartz grip — or handle. . .'

Paula's eyes widened. 'Oh? Why? Was he lame?'

'He was most probably vain — certainly not lame.' Karl's tone was mocking. 'Seriously, though, it was in those days, perhaps, very fashionable to lean on a rose-quartz-handled stick. The rose-quartz would, of course, have come from South-West, as it was known then. You were, a moment ago, speaking about fate. Horst, as a young man, decided to make the military his career, and after entering military service he was sent out here to serve with the Schutztruppe in 1904. At the end of hostilities, in 1907, he returned to Germany, where he married a girl called Hannah, and they came to this country, where he built Sturmvögel. Well, as fate would have it, he was back in Germany when World War One came along and he joined the army once again, and was killed in 1916. The castle which he built, which had been a dream of his, is about to be sold once more—but who knows, perhaps my son will buy it back one day?'

Paula felt her heart sink. 'Oh? You have a son, then?'

'No. But I hope to have a son, naturally. What man doesn't?'

There was a brief silence and then she asked, 'What did you use for light last night—with the generator not working?'

He smiled. 'There are, I discovered, lamps of all descriptions which just have to be filled with this and that, and so there followed another shopping expedition—to Lüderitz this time. I bought as many candles as I could—I don't think there is a candle left in Lüderitz, in fact! I was advised, before leaving Germany, that the generator does not work. There is a borehole which, thanks to a previous owner, does work. According to those diaries we have back home, the availability of water was a big problem for those early settlers. There was, I understand, a pump station some hundred kilometres away and some water was supplied to the town, which was also dependent on barrels of water brought all the way from Cape Town and hauled through the burning sand by two unfortunate mules. Condensers, I believe, were also used to make sea-water drinkable—and so I guess I am lucky after all.'

'*You* sound like the one who should be writing the book!' Paula laughed a little. 'You've done more research than I have. Anyway, I must really be going. I've been working terribly hard lately, but this morning I decided to take the afternoon off. Whenever I get round to thinking about the book, I come out here and walk around and daydream. Sometimes I make notes.'

'I'll be driving into Lüderitz in the near future. Perhaps I could look you up? I'll need to track down artisans.'

On a sudden impulse she said, 'You should give Odd Jobbers a try.'

He showed immediate interest. 'That sounds like an answer to a prayer. Where will I find these people?'

'I might have their card on me.' She began to search in her bag. 'Ah, here you are.'

Looking at the card, which of course was her own, but without her name on it, he said, 'This looks promising. I will either phone them from Lüderitz or call on them when I'm there. There is, of course, no phone here! No phone, no lights, no pleasant company. Don't you feel sorry for me?'

Paula laughed. 'Very sorry — but I'll feel more sorry for myself if I hit a sandstorm on the way back.'

'By the way, apart from researching your book, what do you do in Lüderitz?' he asked.

She was aware of his genuine interest.

'Actually, I'm an architect, but there's nothing in that line for me here, so I take whatever work I can get. . .that's what it really amounts to.'

'An architect, huh? I'm impressed.' He sounded more amused now than impressed, she thought.

'Why is that? Is it because I happen to be a mere woman?' Her low husky voice had cooled.

He laughed softly. 'Yes, I suppose, if I am honest, yes, but I would not say you are a *mere* woman.' The grooves on either side of his mouth kept appearing whenever he laughed or smiled.

'Now I wonder why you found it necessary to say that?' Her angry eyes searched his face. 'Are there no woman architects in Germany?'

'There *are* woman architects, of course. I don't think I would engage one of them, however.'

Although she realised he was goading her, Paula felt a huge resentment.

'Don't make me fed up with your man's sarcasm! When it comes to woman architects, let's change the subject.'

'Well, to change the subject,' his voice was still teasing, 'Namibia must take some getting used to. Are you not homesick?'

Her blue eyes still glittered. 'I'm not actually homesick, although I've felt ready to go back home for some time now. I must confess I do miss the smell of wet grass and foliage. I even find myself craving for perpetually glistening-with-rain pavements. I know one thing — when I do get back home, I'll go mad buying up all the flowers I can lay my hands on. I'll never get enough of them. Now tell me, what did you expect me, as a mere woman, very out of touch at the moment, to answer? That I love being back to back with the biggest and driest desert in the world?'

'As an out of touch architect, at the moment you seem to be flourishing, but then what is it they say — the most rare flowers always bloom in the desert?'

'I'm anything but a rare flower, believe me,' she assured him.

'With your flaming hair and unusual eyes, I should say you are.'

Instantly she was on her guard. 'By the way, did you know that Lüderitz is well known for its rare desert rose?' She stared back at his grey eyes, wondering what lay behind their expression.

'No.' He sounded surprised. 'I can't imagine roses blooming in the desert — but then again, they do have thorns to protect themselves with, so it would appear that you are a typical desert rose.'

Paula laughed. 'They don't bloom in the desert — you have to dig for them. They're formed from gypsum and calcium sulphate salts, which, I'm told, develop under damp conditions. I can only imagine these conditions to be the result of the fog which rolls in from the Atlantic. Actually, when I come to think of it, a desert rose looks something like a crystal rosette, which is exactly what it is. By the way, you can get a permit from the DNC offices and search for them. You're allowed two hours and are allowed three sand roses.'

'And so you must have done this yourself?'

'Yes, I have. I found two.'

He kept his steel-grey eyes on her face. 'This crystal rosette is not, of course, from what you have told me, suitable for a buttonhole?'

'Hardly. Do you enjoy wearing a buttonhole?'

'Only when it comes to weddings — and who knows, I might decide to get married in Namibia?'

Paula felt her eyes flicker. 'Is that possible?'

'It is very possible — as possible as the son I intend to have by my wife one day. Maybe this son will buy Sturmvögel back into the von Buren family.'

'I see. . .' She smiled faintly. 'It sounds interesting — but if I don't leave soon I'll be in trouble. It'll be dark soon.'

A moment later, as they were going down the steps leading from the front door, Paula caught her heel in a large crack which had appeared in the stone and she fell against him. For a heart-stopping second she thought they were both going to fall, then Karl's arms went around her.

As he looked at her, his eyes narrowed slightly. He made her excited in a way she had never felt before, and once again she was aware of the sexual tension between them.

'These steps will have first priority when the

Odd Jobbers arrive,' he said carelessly, as he first steadied and then released her.

At her pick-up he said, 'I'll see you again, of course? Where—in Lüderitz?'

'Oh, I'll drop by one day,' she told him.

He seemed amused by her reaction. 'You don't want *me* to drop in. Is this what you are telling me?'

'It's no secret where I live.' She felt the current between them. 'It's in Pequena Lane, actually, but I do have a very private lifestyle.'

He seemed surprised. 'In Pequena Lane? In that case, you are close to Heinrich?'

'Yes, three doors away.'

'And so you must be number twenty-one, because his is the last cottage?'

Paula started the engine. 'Thanks again for showing me around,' she said.

Karl's grey eyes held hers. 'My pleasure.'

When Paula got back, there was a long letter from home waiting for her. The last of the horses were sold today, wrote her father. 'Practically everything is gone, Paula. I keep asking myself what went wrong—and worse, what next?'

'Well, Dad,' she said aloud, 'I find myself asking exactly the same question. What next?'

Meeting the dashing Count Karl von Buren wasn't at all what she'd expected when she came to Lüderitz. Some silly words came to her mind. . . She was as pure as snow, but she drifted.

CHAPTER TWO

PAULA'S cottage was white with blue window-frames and faced a sand road. There was a low stone wall, and from most of the windows there were views of the deep blue waters of the bay, where the fishing boats were moored. Many of the Lüderitz houses seemed to be growing out of rocks, and a cement ramp had been built over the rocks and sand to the garage belonging to the house across the road. In the distance, a church appeared to be parked on the sand, and at certain times ships at sea looked like the skeletons of ships in the fog.

Without thinking it necessary to seek the advice of the estate agent who had been authorised to let the cottage and to whom she paid the rent, Paula had made several non-structural alterations. Not only had the alterations been in the interest of her own comfort, but they had been a way of keeping her handymen occupied during slack periods. She had also decorated and furnished the cottage on a low budget, for she was, after all, returning to Ireland. By the time she had finished decorating the result was a palette of exciting colour. She had worked on the secondhand furniture and had even successfully disguised crates as tables for lamps by topping them with glass which had been cut into circles and covered with attractive floor-length cloths.

The pictures, arranged in interesting groups, were framed copies of paintings done by an artist friend, Josh Quantril, and had come from one of the calendars produced by him in his studio, Thirstland. These small reproductions depicted scenes of Namibia. . .the desert, Fish River Canyon, Skeleton Coast, seascapes, wild animals in the Etosha National Park and the living fossil plant known as the Welwitschia Mirabilis, found only in the Namib—some of which were estimated to be almost two thousand years old.

Apart from the cottage, she was renting what had once been a small shop, and this was now her office and well lit by the large front window. From here she enjoyed a closer view of the harbour—big tyres fastened against the sea wall, bollards, floats which looked like coloured balls, red buoys in the water, and a crane. Almost golden-coloured nets were piled on the wooden pier or on the decks of fishing vessels. At the present time, a yellow and white vessel called *Windvögel* showed up to disadvantage an incredibly rusty ship.

At the back of the office an outbuilding stood in a small piece of ground, and this set-up was invaluable when it came to storing tools, left-over timber, stone, sand, bricks and cement.

After a particularly hard day, during which she had worked with her handymen, Kobus Fredericks and Johnny Abrahams, Paula had gone to her office to get her books up to date. What was supposed to have been a simple alteration to a small bakery had turned into something resembling a nightmare, she found herself thinking, as she tried to concentrate on her figures. Günther, the owner of the bakery, had wanted the old-fashioned floor tiles lifted so that new tiles could be laid, and, since the existing tiles had been set into a thick, tar-like substance, taking them up had proved both difficult and messy.

When the phone rang, she lifted the receiver with considerable impatience. She was craving for a hot bath — the only way her aching and protesting body and mind could regain some of their equilibrium.

'Hello, Odd Jobbers. Can I help you?' When there was no immediate reply she said again, 'Hello? Odd Jobbers. Can I help you?'

'Yes. I have been given your card. . .'

There was only one man with an attractive accent and voice like that, she thought, and suddenly felt the beating of her heart.

There was another pause and then he went on, 'I am wondering why your voice sounds familiar.'

In her slightly husky voice she answered sweetly, 'Perhaps it's the phone.'

'Perhaps. I wish to see your manager. Is it

possible to come in within — let's say — the next ten minutes? I am in Lüderitz, where I have just about completed a business matter, and this would be suitable to me.'

Paula gave the phone the haughty look which was intended for him. 'I'm afraid it *is* late and the manager is about to leave. The office is closed, actually. What about tomorrow? Will you be in Lüderitz tomorrow? Say about ten? I can fit you in then.'

'I will make a point of being there. Ten will have to do.'

He's used to getting his own way and he's angry, she thought, amused. 'I'll put you down for ten, Mr. . .?'

'Karl von Buren.'

'We'll see you then,' she told him.

As she replaced the receiver, Paula was staggered at his arrogance. I wish to see your manager. . .

Wearing a blue and purple caftan of fine wool, she padded round the cottage the next morning in her bare feet while she prepared and then ate breakfast before going to her wardrobe to look out something glamorous to wear.

Finally she decided on a white shirt, with broad floral bands of lilac and honey down the front, to go with a dusky pink button-through skirt with self-belt and a jacket to match. The outfit was more suited to London than Lüderitz, she thought, smiling a little, but still. . .she didn't often have occasion to dress up. She swept her flaming auburn hair back from her face and knotted it at the back of her head, permitting several carefully careless tendrils to escape and to highlight the style and accentuate her blue eyes. So far as she was concerned, this interview with Karl von Buren was important and she had to look her best. The shock awaiting him would come later.

Directly he walked into her office, she felt the assurance which stemmed from knowing that she still knew how to appear glamorous and sensual when the occasion arose.

'That was foolish, no? After you'd had your fun, why didn't you tell me?' Beneath the dark strokes of his brows his steel-grey eyes were cold.

'Before we start, can I get you some coffee?' she asked, feeling a twinge of guilt now.

'You are evading my question.' He spoke with controlled impatience. 'However, coffee would be — welcome, thank you.'

Before making her way to the cupboard-sized kitchen, Paula slipped out of her dusky pink jacket and draped it behind her chair, and then, gesturing in the direction of the other chair on the opposite side of her desk, she said, 'Do take a seat. I won't be a moment.'

Ignoring her invitation, he went to stand at the window, and her eyes flickered over the charcoal-coloured trousers he was wearing with a T-shirt of the same shade.

After a moment or two she returned with the tray.

'Before we start, let me fill you in,' she said. 'This happens to be my business. In other words, I am the manager.'

Karl turned round and she felt the full power of those intense steel-grey eyes, and suddenly she knew she was running into trouble.

'Why did you have to beat about the bush?' he demanded. 'What is the problem?'

She gave a small annoyed laugh. 'No problem. There was no beating about the bush—it was just a joke!'

For a moment their eyes held. 'Just a joke? Well, as long as you don't waste my time with any more jokes.'

Paula waited for her fury to pass before she answered.

'Now why should I waste your time?' she queried.

'At the risk of certain conflict, I am wondering what exactly you know about the building trade— and I don't happen to be—just joking.' He glanced round and then looked across at her again. 'To my mind, what seems to be missing here are the geraniums in parakeet-pink pots. Look, don't you think that sooner or later somebody is going to ask you what exactly it is you are trying to do?' His tone was sarcastic.

'Let's dispense with the sarcasm, Count von Buren,' she said firmly. 'I'm an architect, and as such I'm qualified to design and supervise the construction of buildings.'

'That still does not make you a builder.' The glimmer of amusement which he permitted himself showed only in the deepening of the grooves in his cheeks. '*No*?'

He came over and took the chair opposite hers, then he leaned back and held her eyes with his own.

Paula passed him his coffee. 'Why should I put up with this? What exactly is it we're trying to convey here? Is it because I'm a woman? Don't you think women are capable of being involved in the building trade?'

'As far as I am concerned, putting building materials together, or merely repairing existing buildings, is not something a woman is capable of supervising.' There was a hint of mockery in his voice. 'Especially an enigmatic, tantalising and totally seductive woman, at that.'

'You surprise me. In other words, *only men* are capable? Is that what you mean?' Her eyes were hostile.

'That is exactly what I mean, but apart from that, I cannot understand why a woman should *want* to start such a business as odd jobbing. It doesn't make sense.'

'Why indeed should it make sense, since you were born lucky and inherited a title?' Oh, why don't you shut up? she asked herself.

'Look,' he laughed softly, 'forget the title. Something is bound to fall down one day—or fall off. Why did you not try something else?'

'This is obviously beyond your comprehension and I don't really have to tell you—but I *did* try, once. I opened a small gallery here. I had to close it down. Although, unlike in the case of the building trade, there was nothing to fall down or fall off, it wasn't paying.' Her eyes were nothing short of fighting mad now.

Karl began to stir his coffee. 'Obviously you stocked the wrong goods, no?'

His remark made her bristle. 'I didn't stock the wrong goods. On the contrary, I stocked anything interesting I could get my hands on.'

He lifted his dark lashes to look at her. 'Such as?'

'Such as gaudy acrylics on canvas, done by a man in Swakomund, drawings and collages inspired by the desert and sent to me by a woman in Windhoek. You name it and I stocked it.'

'That was probably your big mistake.'

Ignoring his sarcasm, she went on, 'I stocked all the so-called tourist traps, don't you see? Until recently, however, there were just not enough tourists—so it was doomed to end up as a nonpaying gallery. Perhaps it would have done better now, since tourism is on the upswing, but at that time I had to begin to think of something else.'

'And this,' he glanced around her office, '*this* — pays?'

'It has its moments. What business doesn't? Now, either we begin to talk business, or you can try somewhere else.' Paula regarded him with displeasure.

'I'll be brief,' he said. 'I am wondering about the staff you employ. How qualified are these people?'

Paula was aware of the irony in his voice, but, for all that, she fell headlong into his trap.

'They're qualified handymen and they happen to be very good. There was a time in their lives when they were fishermen, here in Lüderitz, but they decided to go to Windhoek for a few years, where they became jacks of all trades, learning as they went and gaining a lot of experience.'

'Nevertheless, they are ex-fishermen?' His eyes held hers.

Paula fought to stay calm, but she felt like grabbing a handful of his dark hair and twisting it.

'They are also, as I have just explained, competent handymen. Are you suggesting that they're not? I'm not claiming to be a master builder, for goodness' sake! I'm what the name implies — an odd jobber.'

'Obviously you see things from one angle. I see them from another. However, taking it at your angle—I, as you are aware, require an estimate on repairs and certain alterations to the Castle Sturmvögel. I explained all this to you the other day. Under the circumstances—the fact that you are an architect—you must be in a position to advise accordingly?'

She found his attitude infuriating and looked at him in wide-eyed astonishment.

'I wouldn't be here if I weren't. Obviously, however, you have your doubts, and I'm beginning to have quite a number of my own. For these reasons, you'd better find somebody else to give you a quote. Permit me to point out that you will find this both time-consuming and difficult, but that's your problem, *no*?' She tried to mimic him. 'I don't think I'm prepared. . .'

'Prepared—or qualified?' It was a direct attack.

'You know what I'm going to do?' she asked. 'I'm going to throw you out of here. I'm not prepared to consider working for you.' She stood up. 'What's really bothering you is the fact that this business is owned, and run, by a woman.'

He remained in his chair, from where he gave her a long look.

'Why don't you sit down again? I do find this whole set-up an unusual arrangement—a woman in charge of a gang of men.'

'Well, you would—but I no longer care.' Paula sat down again. 'As I see it, you see everything through a self-satisfied man's eyes.'

'I am, after all, a man,' he mocked. 'You know, I keep wondering what you will say next.'

'Do you?' Paula's patience was taxed to the limit. 'It might interest you to know that I keep wondering the same thing about you. Let me say one more thing, though—you're very much the type of man who thinks, if he's a bachelor, then she's an old maid. If he's married and is jealous and over-possessive, he's a devoted husband, but if she likes to come first in his life, she's the one who's possessive and bitterly jealous. I could go on and on.'

'Don't let me stop you,' he taunted. 'I'll start the ball rolling again—if he's grey, he's silver-haired. If *she* is grey, she's grey. However, perhaps I am missing something. What has all this got to do with the building trade?'

Looking at him, Paula thought how supremely confident he was of ruffling her.

'Perhaps I should have added,' he went on, 'you appear to be the type who is obviously easily excitable and offended. In other words, if *he* remains calm, *she* goes to pieces.'

'I'm not like that at all.' She felt infuriated with herself for not being able to drop the subject.

'No? Judging by your woman's customary form of sarcasm, it would appear that you are, but let's not become sidetracked by all this. Let's drop this nonsense. The point here is—how soon can you come to Sturmvögel to assess the conditions there and, in turn, furnish me with a quote? I am in a hurry to get this project, and other business matters in Lüderitz, over and done with so that I can return to Germany.'

Because she badly needed this job, which could go on for several months, Paula swallowed her pride, but to save her face she decided to hedge.

'I'm under immense pressure at the moment. Not until next week.'

His expression suggested that he did not believe her. 'Not until next week?' he echoed.

'I have other commitments to see to first. Count von Buren, your whole attitude today, your whole tone has done nothing but infuriate me. I would like to point out that I operate the same as any other small business — only better — and I do happen to have other obligations to meet first. It's as simple as that.'

He stood up and looked down at her. 'What day next week?' he asked.

She thought for a moment. 'Wednesday.'

'Shall I drive into Lüderitz to pick you up? And by the way, make it Karl.'

'I have my own transport, which you saw for yourself. Will you be there on Wednesday?' She was still angry and on edge.

'Since I am living there, yes.' The grooves appeared in his cheeks. 'What time shall I expect you, Paula?'

Suddenly drugged with dreams at the way in

which he pronounced her name, she said, without thinking, 'I'll be there at eight — or will you still be in bed at that time?'

She regretted the words immediately.

'I could make a point of *being* in bed.' A new element had entered into their conversation and his voice contained sexy mockery. 'But I'll probably be on the beach.' He got to his feet. 'And so, after all that, you did not have to throw me out.' He laughed softly. 'What kind of remark was that? I could pick you up with my little finger. Maybe, one day, I will show you.'

'You'd regret it, I can assure you,' she told him.

'What exactly would you do?' he drawled.

'Bite and kick. Pull your hair. Hit you. . .'

'Like a typical woman, in fact?'

After a pause she said, 'I *am*, after all, a woman.'

His grey eyes went over her. 'That had not escaped me, one way and another. Until Wednesday, then, when we'll meet things head-on — and to the contract which could follow.'

The beach was where Paula found Karl on the day she arrived at the castle, walking slowly and easily towards her. When he waved, she did not wave back.

Gulls and cormorants skimmed the waves and filled the air with their cries. As Karl drew level with where she was standing beside the pick-up, which she had parked in front of the exterior walls and steps, her eyes flickered over him. He was wearing nothing but white shorts, and the dark hairs on his chest and forearms glistened in the waves of sun which were now filtering through the morning fog.

Shoving his dark hair back from his forehead, he said, 'Good morning. As you can see, I am very much up and about.'

'Hi.' It took an effort on her part to sound offhand.

'How are you?' His voice was friendly and intimate.

She shrugged. 'So-so.'

'Have you had breakfast?' he asked.

'A long time ago.'

I could fall in love with this man, she was thinking, as he gave her another disarming smile.

'To undo the damage of several days ago, I was hoping you would have breakfast with me,' he went on. 'I got up early and drove into Lüderitz where, among a few other items, I bought crois- sants from Günther's Bakery. I could also have offered you fruit juice — from a can, of course — and coffee.'

'Coffee would be nice,' she answered, suddenly looking forward to it. 'Tell me, what did you think of the floor?'

Karl seemed puzzled. 'The floor?' he queried.

'The floor — at Günther's?'

'Oh, yes. I remember thinking the tiles were very attractive.'

'And attractively laid?' Paula persisted.

'That goes without saying, because of course you are going to tell me that this was done by Odd Jobbers, no?'

'So there you go, then. I must admit I was hoping you'd remark on the floor of your own accord, though.' She laughed a little.

'Seriously, I *did* notice it!' Something in his voice told her that he was not entirely serious.

'I don't believe you, but still. . .' She shrugged.

'It's true.' His eyes were teasing.

They began to walk towards the castle which, except for those low, retaining exterior walls which served to control the sand, had nothing to guard its privacy.

'You should get two stone lions to guard the entrance,' Paula suggested jokingly, to make conversation.

He turned to look at her. 'On the one side a bachelor lion, with a silver mane, and on the other side, a grey-haired old-maid lioness?'

'Analysed, that means you're not going to let up on what I said the other day.'

'I never let up,' he answered, pushing open the massive door. 'By the way, Paula, you are looking very efficient.' His eyes went over the glazed cotton khaki trousers she was wearing with a jacket of the same colour. Her hair was swept back in a chic

French twist, and turquoise earrings accentuated the colour of her eyes, even down to the tiny flecks which appeared in them.

'Thank you. It just so happens that I'm as efficient as I look.' There was an edge to her voice, now, as she was made aware that she was defending herself, when she had no need to.

As they entered the big hall Karl said, 'Make yourself comfortable, while I go and put on a shirt. Wander about, if you like—but not through there.' His eyes went to a room leading off the hall.

'Why? Is it haunted?' she asked lightly.

'No. It happens to be the *Herrenzimmer*, which is a room reserved for men. It only came to my mind yesterday. This room was mentioned in Horst's notes. Last night I was going through some of the things I had brought with me and came upon the original plans of Sturmvögel, and there it was. . . *Herrenzimmer*.'

'Now I know who you take after,' Paula mocked. 'In his intense support of male domination, he must have given your great-grandmother a hard time.'

'Oh, I wouldn't say that. From what I have gathered, Horst was very much in love with Hannah. In other words, he was a devoted husband.'

'Which would have made her a possessive and jealous wife, I suppose?'

She was looking at the panelling in the sitting-room when Karl returned, buttoning the shirt which he had obviously just flung on over his white shorts. He was wearing canvas espadrilles and Paula could imagine him on some geranium-terraced villa on the Mediterranean.

'After breakfast we can look around and I will let you know what I have in mind here. One thing, Paula——'

'Yes?' She waited for him to tell her.

'I take it you will be able to deal successfully, when it comes to ordering the necessary materials for these repairs and alterations?'

She could not believe her ears and, immediately on her high horse, she retorted, 'If I don't know by now, how will I ever know? I've coped up to now—and by the way, I'll probably come up with a few suggestions of my own.'

'And I will, of course, give you my undivided attention.' His grey eyes were amused.

There was something in the way Karl von Buren moved that Paula found exciting. There was an easy animal sensuality about him. His eyes, steel-grey, were often calculating and watching, and his voice had authority. . .the kind of authority she secretly looked for in a man. An authority which was lacking in Josh Quantril, the current male in her life!

'. . .let me know what you think,' Karl was saying.

'I'm — sorry?' She felt confused, since she hadn't been listening to him.

'I suggested we sit outside — but it is up to you.'

'That sounds — nice. It's not often I get the chance to sit and look at the Atlantic.'

He had, she saw, placed a small round table and two chairs next to one of the low walls. She sat down and gazed in the direction of the sea, and was immediately struck by the fact that both their great-grandfathers, not to mention Karl's great-grandmother, Hannah, had gazed out on this same sea — and probably even swum in it.

As he leaned back in his chair, Karl's grey gaze followed her own. 'It was a long time ago,' he said, sensing her thoughts, 'but it's still the same.'

'Yes, much is still the same, I'm sure. Now that I'm in Namibia, I can see that it would not have taken all that much to get lost in the desert and to have come to an untimely death — especially in those days. That is, I feel sure, what must have happened to my great-grandfather, Rory. I was reading just the other day about a Father Julian who went off in the sixth century to convert. . .' Paula lifted her shoulders '. . .anyone he could find, I guess. Anyway, the climate in the Sahara was so hot and appalling that he used to sit, wearing nothing but a linen garment of some sort, in caves full of water.' She laughed a little. 'Don't ask me where the water in the caves came from, but there he sat, from nine to four every day. Presumably he had a watch.'

'I find myself wondering how many souls the good Father Julian managed to convert before nine in the morning and then again after four — presumably he *did* have a watch? — in the afternoon,' Karl remarked drily, and they both laughed.

'It just goes to show the heat, though, in a desert,' Paula said.

There was a short silence and then Karl went on, 'I'm interested; surely you should continue with the research on your book by venturing further afield than Lüderitz?'

'Like the good Father Julian?' she mocked. 'What's the point of venturing further afield? Rory Stewart came to Lüderitz and the surrounding area, after all. Up until the time he disappeared, this is where he appears to have been working.'

'And yet you have mentioned that he might have left Lüderitz and ended up getting lost, no? In other words, Paula, what I am trying to say is that in order to stimulate your imagination you should travel about more.' He looked at her in a way that she found frankly disturbing. 'What are we going to do about this?'

As their eyes met and held for a moment, she felt the dangerous excitement of him. What was he suggesting? She was thrown only for a moment. 'My research has come to a full stop, I'm afraid. It's ironic, but since I've come here I've spoken to people about the history of Sturmvögel in an attempt to find out what might have happened to him. All I have come up with is what happened to George Pond of London, the boots of a man who rode out on a camel and were found twenty years later, when the dune which had been covering his body shifted, and various remittance men from Germany. So you see, everything, in fact, except what happened to Rory Paul Stewart.' She reached for her coffee mug and sat back. 'I've always been too busy to take time off to arrange anything. There are tours, of course. There's someone who takes people out to the desert in a Land Rover, where a car can't possibly go.' She crossed her long trousered legs and saw Karl's eyes go to them.

'Might I remind you that *I* have a Land Rover?' His tone was a challenge, which she picked up immediately.

'Let me understand this. What exactly are you talking about?' She tried to get her excited feelings under control.

'I am inviting you to drive out into the desert with me—where no car can possibly go. Think about it.'

She swung one slim, trousered leg. 'To get the feel of the place for my book, I take it?'

'What else?' His eyes held hers.

It suddenly struck her what a solitary life she led, locked in through lack of money, with the Atlantic on one side and the desert on the other.

'I'll think about it.' Her voice was cool. 'I don't think so, though. I just haven't the time.'

'*Make* time.' He watched her with confident eyes.

He had just about finished his breakfast when Paula delved into her bag and took out a notebook and a ballpoint pen. She lifted her lashes to look at him. 'By the way, you can't just drive about at random. Often permits are required,' she told him.

'So. . .I will make arrangements to obtain the necessary permits. Simple.'

For a moment she allowed him to go on searching her eyes, then she stood up and went to stand beside the wall, waiting for him.

For the next two hours they looked over the castle and discussed the repairs and certain alterations which had to be carried out.

Since Paula's great-grandfather had been a carpenter here, she was interested in the woodwork — the beamed ceilings, for instance, the panelling and the great wooden staircase. She also gave herself up to the luxurious feeling that, if Karl approved of her quote, she would have work here for the next three months at least. It could be a spell of exquisite escapism from money problems. Suddenly the urge to go back home to Ireland did not seem as great as it had been before she had met Karl von Buren. She tried to crush these feelings immediately. After all, there was probably a woman in his life. He *had* hinted at marriage when they had discussed desert roses. Maybe he had plans for sending for her and being married at Sturmvögel — for sentimental reasons — before he opened it to the public and then, as a worthwhile investment, it was sold once again.

Cutting into her thoughts, Karl said, 'I have been watching you. Part of you is so very far away. What were you thinking about?'

On a light, artificial tone she said, 'I shouldn't really tell you this, but I was wondering whether you're planning to be married in the castle after it's been restored. You sounded, the other day, as though this might be on the cards and a beautiful fiancée would be coming to Namibia — along with other members of your family, for the wedding. . .'

He laughed. 'I can see why you are going to write! You have a vivid imagination. There have always been other things I'd rather do than have a fiancée.'

'Oh?' She tried to sound very casual. 'Such as? Or shouldn't I ask?' Laughing a little, she added, 'I don't suppose you'll tell me, anyway.'

'Sooner or later,' he mocked back, 'I suppose I will have to lie to you, but right now I'll admit I prefer skiing down the snow-capped Alpine slopes, driving fast cars, flying, travelling. . . However, when it comes to being involved with beautiful women, let's just say I like to be involved — but not too involved.' Although he was teasing, he spoke with a disturbing directness. 'Is this what you wanted to hear?'

Paula tried not to sound involved herself, but she felt unaccountably depressed, just the same.

'Quite the opposite, in fact. I was hoping to hear that you're a man of sober and quiet character, since I might be working for you. . .you know, chairman of your local committee back home or something—someone who plans campaigns. Don't you take time off to work?'

'For sure—I work very hard. I'm a designer, for one thing. I design fast cars. Apart from that, along with my good mother, I run the *schloss* which, for economic reasons, is open to the public seven months of the year.'

'And the *schloss*? Where is it—Karl?' Using his name gave her an odd little thrill.

'It is in northern Bavaria and, situated as it is in a thickly wooded valley, it is one of the few castles to make it in its original form. What is so remarkable is that it has never, thank God, experienced conflict in any form—even during the Second World War.'

'That's wonderful. Is that because it's situated in such a remote area?' she asked.

'Yes. The fact that the walls are very thick and that there is also a moat had nothing to do with it. What we do have to thank is its geographical location. My mother lives in a small wing. . .'

'What do you call a *small* wing?' she cut in, laughing.

'Well,' his smile was totally disarming, '*small*. My sister, her husband and two small children live in another wing. There are countless dogs and a couple of well-brushed, well-fed cats. It is nothing like this place. For one thing, it's pink!'

'Oh, you make me jealous. How romantic!'

'I agree—it is very romantic. My great-grand-father obviously did not base Sturmvögel on a Bavarian *schloss*—but then everything is opposite here. No snow, for instance, huh? You know, in the winter, at home, we are virtually imprisoned. We are practically buried in snow. Inside, though, we are all very warm and comfortable.'

'You must have quite a family tree?' queried Paula.

He laughed a little. 'About five hundred years of growth, that we're absolutely sure of, anyway.' Their eyes met. 'And you?'

She sighed. 'You're the one whose life seems to be tinged with pink romance. I may be on the doorstep of the desert, but my father is the one who's crossing a desolate plain right now.'

Karl showed immediate interest. 'How is this?'

'He's become bankrupt. . .horses sold, stables closed. The news came as quite a shock to me. Well, not quite a shock—a terrible shock! I walked around feeling stunned for days.' As she spoke, she thought she could have told Karl that this news from Ireland had meant that she had found herself stranded in Namibia and, in the circumstances, would not dream of asking her father for a loan. 'I had no idea all this was happening,' she went on. 'By the grace of God, he appears to be hanging on to the house, which is rather lovely, but he's utterly defeated—something unusual for him.'

'But quite understandable.' Karl's voice was warm and intimate. 'I am sorry to hear this.'

She shrugged. 'It's just one of those things, I guess. Well, I'll look into all this,' she tapped her notebook with her pen, 'and get back to you with my estimate.'

'Tell me,' he said quietly, 'who waits for you in Ireland?'

Realising what he was getting at, she said lightly, 'My father.'

'I realise your father—but I'm serious. Who else?'

'Friends, of course.' As she looked at him, Paula had the feeling that, as a man who liked to be involved, but not seriously involved, now he'd met her he was not going to be content with anything less than getting her into bed with him.

'In particular?' His steel-grey eyes challenged her.

'In particular—several frightfully handsome, intelligent men who will no doubt be pleased to see me again when I get back home.'

'And in the meantime, in Lüderitz?'

'In the meantime, in Lüderitz, a frightfully handsome artist who takes me to dinner from time to time. Is that what *you* wanted to hear?' she mocked.

'I am concerned about your father, of course, but on the other hand, you'd better do some thinking about the frightfully handsome artist in Lüderitz, who takes you to dinner from time to time. Where else does he take you?'

Paula laughed. 'In *Lüderitz*? We swim, sometimes in the sea and sometimes in the pool at one of the hotels. We often spend time enjoying the open spaces — or rather I do, while he sketches.'

'Well, the focus of nature in Namibia is on wild animals, I understand. And so you must have gone away together to explore such places as the vast shallow depression known as the Etosha Park, which is some distance from here?'

'What kind of question is that? That I go away with Josh?' She regarded him with cool eyes.

'*Josh*, huh?' He gave her a long look and then smiled. 'It never occurred to me.'

'I haven't been to the Etosha Pan with Josh,' said Paula, 'but I hope to go before going back to Ireland. The most we see, Josh and I, are beetles and lizards scurrying about the shifting sands just outside Lüderitz. Well,' she glanced at her watch, 'I believe we've covered everything, so I really must be off.'

'There is one other thing ——' began Karl.

'Somehow I thought there might be. What is it?'
She spoke on a light, teasing note.

'To celebrate, have lunch with me in Lüderitz.'

'Lunch would be nice, of course, but we haven't
anything to celebrate — not yet, anyway. You might
not approve of my quote. Unfortunately, though, I
have work to do. I'll get back to you.'

Karl walked with her to her pick-up.

'Drive carefully,' he told her.

'I always do. I'm a very careful person, actually.'
She gave him a direct look.

'Women are rarely careful drivers,' he mocked.

'Oh, that's just not true and you know it! I'll tell
you one thing, women seldom take their frustrations, or anger, out on a car.'

'Men don't have frustrations.'

She laughed. 'Do you honestly believe that?
What about my father, at this very moment, for
one?'

'Men are too smart to become frustrated. They
always come up with something,' he assured her.

Paula opened the door and slid into the seat.
'Keep an open mind,' she teased. 'You can't
be sure.'

CHAPTER THREE

MOST days began with fog which swept from the Atlantic into the desert, bringing life-giving moisture to plants and animals. Today, thought Paula, was no exception.

Karl von Buren had approved of her quotation with regard to the work to be done on the Castle Sturmvögel and during that time she had seen him three times. Once they'd met for lunch at Otto's seafood restaurant and the other two occasions had been strictly business, and both these business meetings took place at the castle.

She was on her way to pick up her handymen, Johnny Abrahams and Kobus Fredericks who, she knew, would be waiting outside their respective cottages.

As she drove, she kept glancing at the mist-shrouded Art Nouveau and Imperial-style buildings, and found herself thinking about a man named Adolf Lüderitz, a Bremen merchant who had begun trading on this exposed spot between the hot Namib dunes and the cold Atlantic Ocean. Lüderitz, the first German settlement in South-West Africa, was named after this man who had managed to persuade Bismarck to place the territory under German protection in 1884.

The thing which really interested Paula, though, was that Adolf Lüderitz, along with a companion, had tragically disappeared under the waves of the Atlantic—which was yet another dismal reminder of how men were lost in those days.

Karl was standing on the steps outside the castle when she arrived, and Paula introduced him to the handymen, who lost no time in lifting the cement-mixer from the pick-up. For a moment or two Karl watched them with moody grey eyes, then he turned to look at Paula.

'Enlighten me, Paula.' He used her name with a flick of contempt, she thought. 'I don't understand.' His eyes swept right over her. 'Why are you dressed like this?'

Fully realising that he was referring to her clean but paint-stained jeans, shirt and denim hat which protected her hair from dust, she said coolly, 'Enlighten *me*, Karl. Like *what*?'

He lifted his shoulders and she could see that for once he was searching for words.

'You want it straight?'

She began to bristle. 'Yes.'

'Well, like a person who spends his working days spreading paint around walls—someone employed by some building contractor. . .'

'I guess that figures, Karl, since I *do* spread paint

around walls from time to time. Does that bother
you?'

'I'll say it bothers me! In fact, it comes as a shock
to see you looking so—unfeminine. There is no
other word for it.'

She hated him intensely at that moment. 'Really?
There's nothing unfeminine about me, Karl. I
happen to take my femininity very seriously, as it
happens. Just remember that, will you, when
you're handing out insults? However, since I don't
devote my life to charity and I'm here to work, I
could hardly be expected to turn up wearing some
narrow black creation and high-heeled sandals,
could I?'

'You go to extremes,' he snapped. 'About working—with these men—I hope you are deceiving
me?'

'I'm not. I've never deceived you.'

'What?' He practically shouted the word at her.
'You have never deceived me? What then do you
call this? I expected you, in your capacity as an
architect, to supervise work here, but. . .'

'I happen to run an Odd Jobbers business,' Paula
cut in, 'and in between running my office, that's
exactly what I am—an odd jobber.'

'Having you turn up here looking like some
plasterer, painter. . .what have you. . .is not what
I was led to expect. Why was I not told about this
state of affairs from the beginning? I'll tell you

why. You entered into this contract with unscrupu-
lous calculation.'

They were both quiet for a moment, looking at
each other furiously.

'What difference would it have made if I *had* told
you?' asked Paula.

'It would have made all the difference in the
world. Do you want me to tell you how this is
going to end?'

Paula stared back at him with glittering blue
eyes. 'I'd be interested to know, naturally.'

'If this is the position, I can't let you have this
contract,' he said coldly.

She felt as if someone had just whitewashed her
face and knew she had gone pale.

'You don't mean that! You *can't*!' How could I
have thought I could ever fall in love with this
man? she thought.

'I do mean it!' He looked at her without understanding — without feeling.

'You must be joking! You take up hours. . .
days. . .weeks of my time and then you stand
there and tell me you can't let me have the contract?' She lifted her shoulders in despair. 'Karl,
during the past few weeks I've ordered all the
building material for this contract. I've even turned
down another job.'

The job to which she referred was neither here
nor there, simply that of adding another shelf to
Josh Quantril's studio, Thirstland, and one which

could be slotted in at any time. What was more, knowing Josh as she did, it was unlikely that she would receive payment for it.

'That's your problem, no?' snapped Karl.

'I wouldn't be too sure if I were you. I don't think it *is* my problem. In fact, what *is* the problem? There is no problem, except in your mind. We have a contract and I mean to keep to it, and if it's the last thing I do I intend to see that *you* also stick to it.'

If you've turned down another job, get it back! I am sure you can manage to inveigle the party concerned. Don't come wheedling and crying to me, Paula.'

'Your male superiority infuriates me!' she continued furiously. 'Are you honestly telling me to forget the whole thing? You can't hire my services just to tell me — *before I even start* — that you've changed your mind!'

'Can't I? Just you try me! Paula,' Karl's steel-grey eyes resembled the Atlantic Ocean just before a gigantic storm, 'if I am going to see a lot of you over the next few months, it is definitely not going to be with you on your knees or up a ladder or hanging over that cement-mixer back there. I have no intention of employing some markedly masculine freak of nature.'

Her first automatic impulse was to slap his face, but she managed to control herself. 'You're overlooking one important factor, Karl. You *have* employed me! If you break, or try to break, this contract, I'll take you to the cleaners, and that's a fact! Think about it! Another thing—and think about this—there's nothing, I repeat nothing *markedly masculine about me!*'

'If you are determined to work here, we will have to remind you of that, no?' His eyes swept right over her. 'Look, I know there is nothing masculine about you. Forget I said it. I meant. . .'

'I know what you meant. I'll sue you, Karl!'

'I said forget that remark. It was said in the heat of the moment.' His voice had risen. 'If we are to keep to this contract, you had better just stay out of my way, because believe me, Paula, when I say that I will go out of my way to prove just how feminine you really are—just how fragile. This is no work for you to be doing.'

'Are you threatening me?' Her voice had also risen.

'No, not threatening. I am making you a promise. I will not hesitate to remind you that you are very much a woman.'

'But that is some kind of threat, surely?'

'It will depend on how you look upon it.' His eyes held hers for a long moment.

In a tight voice she said, 'I'm beginning to understand you, and what I'm beginning to understand, I don't like.'

A few minutes later she was driving recklessly back to Lüderitz, leaving Kobus and Johnny to get on with the repairs to the outside steps. All she could think of were Karl's steel-grey eyes going over her.

In an effort to calm herself she went to her cottage, only to find that an upsetting letter from the estate agent awaited her in which she was advised that the cottage was to be sold and she was therefore being given three months' notice in which to make the necessary arrangements to vacate it. For his part, the letter continued, Count von Buren regretted any inconvenience which might be encountered.

Stunned, Paula read the letter a second time, but there it was. . . Count van Buren regrets. . .

So this was why Karl had seemed so surprised when he had discovered that she lived in Pequena Lane? Why hadn't he come into the open and told her that the cottage belonged to the von Buren family?

On the spur of the moment and seething with rage, she decided to call on Josh before returning to the Castle Sturmvögel.

Josh was surprised to see her. 'I thought you'd started work at the famous fortress?' he queried.

'I've started, but I had to come back to Lüderitz for something,' she explained.

Josh went on painting. 'Well, I'm not complaining. Tell me, how do you like this barium yellow? I'm using a little here and there in the right direction to highlight these leaves.'

'It certainly does just that.' Paula's moody eyes went over him when he wasn't looking.

As an artist, Josh had a natural eye for beauty, but appearances meant nothing to him, and as usual he was looking anything but presentable. His jeans were only fit for the rubbish bin, she thought critically. He was not wearing a shirt, but for some reason known only to himself he was wearing a red scarf. The espadrilles on his feet were just about falling apart. She supposed this was how *she* must have appeared to Karl earlier on, and she took an unsettled breath.

Josh's studio smelled of oils and white spirit, and these smells mingled with the salty tang of the sea that drifted in through the windows. Paula gazed despondently at the noisy seagulls and many cormorants, as they swooped through the sky, skimmed the wavetops and flew over the anchored boats that rocked in the harbour. There was a special atmosphere about Lüderitz, she thought. There was nothing complicated about the place — that was, until now. . . She turned again, to look at Josh, who was painting the plant known as the Welwitschia Mirabilis.

'Josh, where do you want that shelf to go?'

'Just something to go up over there.' He gesticulated with his brush. 'Nothing elaborate.'

Paula watched him as he put his brush down and came over to where she was standing. When he made to take her in his arms she said, 'No! I— look—a sight.'

'I happen to like you looking like this,' he told her, and reached for her denim hat and took it off and dropped it on a nearby stool. Her auburn hair immediately fell into a smooth, elegant style all of its own. Then his arms closed about her again. 'I'd rather have you looking like this than looking self-orientated, sulky and very expensively pampered.'

In recent months Paula had come to realise that she was lonely and to recognise the desire she felt to be made love to. Sometimes this was like an undeniable hunger, but although she had grown fond of Josh Quantril, she was aware of his many weaknesses and had no intention of becoming seriously involved with him. With his fair hair and pale blue eyes, he was attractive in a drop-out kind of way, and it would have been the easiest thing in the world to let him make love to her.

His mouth sought hers and, in the angry and reckless mood she was in, she felt her blood begin to race and she clung to him in quick response.

When Josh's arms slackened and fell away, her eyes opened and widened, and then she saw the reason. Karl von Buren was standing just inside the studio.

'I'm sorry, I seem to have interrupted something.' There was an abundance of meaning in his voice as his forbidding grey eyes went right over Paula.

'Look, it's not a problem.' Josh's manner was easy and confident. 'You just caught me kissing my lady-love. What can I do for you?'

Completely ignoring Josh, Karl went on looking at Paula, taking her apart with his steel-grey eyes.

'Heinrich seemed to think I'd find you here,' he said.

Paula's blue eyes reflected her anger. 'Really? You've been busy tracking me down, in other words? And what gives Herr Heinrich the right to guess where I'd be?'

'Look,' Karl told her, 'I happened to be in Lüderitz on business, which as it happens involved Heinrich. I went to your cottage and found you out. . .'

'And then you went back to Herr Heinrich's and put out a few feelers, is that it? What's so important, anyway?'

Karl's laugh was sarcastic. 'What is important is that when I left the castle your ex-fishermen were dead to the world. That is what is so important, since it involves our contract—but we'll discuss this outside.'

As Paula watched him leave, she wondered how she could cope with such overwhelming anger without making a fishwife of herself.

'Who the hell does he think he is?' Josh's usually placid voice contained annoyance. 'Is that the famous Count?'

Paula grabbed her denim hat. 'Yes — and I'll soon sort him out, believe me!'

Her small pick-up was parked outside Josh's studio and Karl's Land Rover stood directly in front of it. With arms crossed, he was leaning against it, and as she approached he straightened and their eyes met in angry combat.

'Don't you think you're carrying things a little far?' asked Paula. 'Tracking me down like this, and then having the audacity to barge into Josh's studio without even bothering to knock?'

'Since, Paula, there happens to be a ceramic tile outside the door which reads "Feel free: walk right in and browse", I felt free to do just that. . .walk right in. I saw no reason to knock. How was anyone to know they would find the architect and the drop-out artist engaged in a moment of wild passion?'

'Let's get to the point, Karl. In the first place, Josh is not a drop-out. He's a little eccentric, maybe, but that's all. Sometimes, when he's busy on something, he doesn't go to bed. He works all night. He's also a very nice person. When he's not satisfied with what he's set out to do, and even if it happens to be very good, in fact, he either sells it to some tourist for next to nothing, or he gives it away.'

'I see. Well, there is obviously a sharing of emotions between you. From your summary, it is plain that you share his untidy habitat with him from time to time.' Karl kept his grey eyes on her face.

'How dare you jump to conclusions?' Paula snapped. 'I *know*, because he's *told* me. I won't have you dragging him down like this. Anyway, Josh is none of your business. . .'

'In that case, I suggest you *do* get to the point! I am referring, Paula, to our contract.'

'Did you go to all this trouble just to let me know that my handymen are having a break?' she demanded.

'Yes, that is exactly what they are having—a suspension of labour—call it anything you like. The fact is that I left them fast asleep on the beach.'

'They always take a nap during tea and lunch,' she retorted angrily. 'They're entitled to these *suspensions of labour*. What's more, they'd go straight to their union if they were stopped. Apart from that, they're quite possibly waiting for me to OK their next job. They must have finished the steps. Have they?'

Karl's steely grey eyes raked her face. 'That is for you to find out, no? Why don't you get back to see for yourself? I realise it must be upsetting for you to be working out of town—that is, when you are not on your boyfriend's doorstep—but since you are determined to see this contract through you'd better start adjusting.'

'Your behaviour is insulting, but, as you say, I'm determined to see this contract through, Karl, and we seem to be stuck with each other. I suggest, therefore, that you run your affairs and I'll run mine—even though I now find myself in the position of having to find another cottage. Why didn't you tell me from the beginning that the cottage belonged to your family? When I told you I lived in Pequena Lane you even worked out what number it would be, since Herr Heinrich's was at the end of the lane. You never cease to amaze me, Karl. That was being totally secretive. You preferred to send me a letter.'

'A letter? What goes on here?' He raked his fingers through his dark hair. 'I particularly issued instructions that you were not to be given notice until *I* authorised it. Have you ever asked yourself, though, how it is you were able to rent that cottage without signing a lease?'

For a moment Paula was confused. 'The estate agent didn't *ask* me to sign a lease.'

'Well, permit me to put you into the picture. When the previous tenants decided to walk out—breaking their lease—the estate agent took it upon herself to let you have the cottage under their name. So far as she was concerned, this saved a lot of bother all round. So far as my mother was concerned, the cottage was under their name, and so far as *I* was concerned it was under their name. In other words, you were paying rent under the name of these people—these previous tenants. I found out, by chance, as you well know, that you were living in one of the four properties belonging to my mother.'

'I don't care what you say, Karl, you *must* have authorised that letter,' she persisted.

'I didn't! It is up to you whether you believe me or not. My instructions were not to give you notice until I had found you a suitable cottage. These instructions have been disregarded, and I intend to look into this.'

'Oh, go to hell! I'll find my own cottage!' When she made to turn away from him, he reached out and grabbed her wrist. His fingers were hard and he held her tightly.

'I haven't finished talking.' His voice had an unpleasant edge to it.

For a moment Paula stared back at him with helpless anger, then she looked down at his fingers.

'Kindly remove your fingers from my wrist!' she hissed.

Ignoring her request, Karl went on, 'But to get back to the work which is to take place at the castle. What happened between you and this man means nothing to me personally. It means nothing to me what you do in your hours of leisure, but what goes on when it comes to our contract is of prime importance. Do you get that?'

'And that's what you wanted to say when you tracked me down today?'

'Yes.' His eyes held hers.

'And yet you wanted to break that very contract before I left the castle today! Didn't you?'

'Look, why don't you employ a foreman?' Karl went on. 'Someone to keep a check on these individuals?'

'I said let go of my wrist!' Paula's blue eyes were beginning to spark. 'You seem to have forgotten.'

He almost flung her hand from him, and she watched him as he turned and opened the door to the Land Rover. He did not get in right away, however.

'By the looks of things, Paula, you are easily pleased. . .judging by the ambitious artist back there. I, on the other hand, am not! It will save us both a lot of time and energy if you remember this.'

'Tell me something,' she said, 'has Herr Heinrich been given notice to vacate his cottage?'

'Yes.'

'I — see. . . And the curio shop? He always told me that the curio shop and his cottage belonged to the same family.'

'The curio shop goes too. It is being sold.'

'So it goes too? Along with poor old Herr Heinrich! Do you think that's fair? You came a long way to smash people. In other words, there would have been time to let us all know well in advance, surely? What's Heinrich going to do for a living now?' Paula demanded.

Karl took an impatient breath. 'Heinrich has known for considerable time now. He was given ample notice.'

'Whereas *I* wasn't!' Her temper was beginning to take over. It was her turn, now, to take *him* apart with her eyes. 'Apart from everything, do you realise how hard I've worked in that cottage? I've made a number of alterations. I've *spent money!*' She felt suddenly drained of energy.

'You have made a number of alterations? You have spent money? With whose permission, Paula?' There was a hard edge to Karl's voice. 'With whose permission did you make these alterations?'

For a moment she was shocked into silence, then she said, 'I didn't think I'd need permission. After all, they weren't structural changes, merely cosmetic. What was wrong with that?'

'What was wrong with that?' he repeated. 'You are a bigger fool than I thought, that is what is wrong.' He took a breath and expelled it angrily. 'That cottage did not belong to you.'

Paula suddenly regretted her rashness in telling him.

'Oh, Karl, what does it matter? I spent money. That's that.'

'What matters is that you attack me like some angry Irish washerwoman. You had no right to make alterations to the cottage. What expenses you incurred and what trouble you went to have nothing to do with me. Do you expect me to feel guilty because I came to Namibia to sell Sturmvögel and the cottages?'

As he got into the Land Rover and slammed the door, Paula tried to restrain herself from shouting after him, but failed.

'I'll vacate that cottage when it suits me, and I'll find another cottage — without any help from you!'

A week went by, and Paula still seethed with anger whenever she thought about the letter from the estate agent and the scene which had taken place outside Josh's studio. As a result, she did her best to avoid Karl as much as possible.

After more days of activity, the steps along with several outside retaining walls had been successfully repaired, but a new problem now presented itself. The cement on hand had come to an end. Impatiently, Paula checked with the suppliers who, in turn, were losing patience with her.

There was little time to think about her great-grandfather who for some reason had deserted his wife and children but had never been — or placed himself — in a position to defend himself.

Working in the Castle Sturmvögel, Paula thought dismally, was not all she had imagined it would be.

Looking fit, tanned and incredibly handsome, Karl was always busy, with the help of a man he had employed by the name of Cecil Peters. Mostly this work seemed to revolve around moving much of the furniture into rooms which were not being worked on at the present time, or coming up next.

Karl's attitude bordered on hostility, and Paula tried to convince herself that this did not bother her, but at the end of a tiring day, she would drive back to Lüderitz feeling ready to break.

Discussions with Karl were always necessary, and during these discussions she was always acutely aware of him. . .his easy strength and the male elegance and grace about him, even when he was wearing nothing else but white or denim shorts.

They were discussing work on one of the embellished fireplaces, and as usual Karl appeared to be in a bad mood.

'Judging by the dust and crumbling stone which has made its way down here, something will have to be done about all the fireplaces soon. We can't wait,' he declared.

'I'm quite aware of that,' Paula responded with an impatience and anger she could not hide. 'The fireplaces were all mentioned in my quotation.'

'So they were,' he snapped, 'but a lot has changed since then. As I see things now, the fireplaces must take first preference. They are, however, but a few of the many problems we have here.'

'For — instance?' Her voice went cold now.

'For instance, I find myself asking one important question, and that is — have you no awareness of your own limitations? All this,' he gestured widely, 'is too much for you. I see it every day. I see you — *as a woman* — flagging. This was a bad idea. I had no idea that you were going to slave here, along with these men.'

These men, or ex-fishermen or individuals, as Karl often referred to Johnny and Kobus, were taking a lunch break, and from where they were standing Paula and Karl could see the handymen sprawled out on the beach. Beside each man there was a plastic lunch-box and a flask. The Atlantic seemed to be breathing heavily and the breeze coming from it was cool. Only the hot, stark and merciless desert, so near to the beach, lay in wait for anyone who dared to venture there.

'Why don't *you* ever break for lunch?' Karl's voice went on impatiently. 'Why is it you go on working while they eat lunch, drink coffee and then pass out on the beach?'

'Because I don't happen to eat lunch, that's why!' Paula had to fight her temper.

'Well, from tomorrow, you *will* eat lunch, and this is an order, because I intend to see to it that you do, and that you also take a break at tea or coffee time.'

'I have no intention of doing that, so just save your breath, Karl.'

'The trouble with you,' he went on impatiently, 'is that you resent authority.'

'Whose authority, Karl? Don't tell me. . .*yours*?

If only you knew how it infuriates me to have you interfering with our work here. Discussing work is something I can cope with, but. . . Look, Karl, I've never walked out on a job yet. Is that what you want me to do — walk out? Is this what you've been aiming at — day in and day out? This is all because I'm a woman!'

He surveyed her with angry disdain. 'You have forgotten what it is to be a woman. I threatened to remind you of that one day. Maybe the time is ripe for me to do just that, huh? I have thought of little else, in fact.' His grey eyes travelled the length of her.

'I don't need you to remind me I'm a woman!' Her eyes were blazing now.

'No? Maybe the artist sees nothing wrong about you looking like some stevedore. I, on the other hand, find you a bothersome presence.'

Before she knew what was happening, he had caught her by the shoulders and drawn her roughly into his arms. For a moment she fought him, and then, instead of feeling the anger she had expected, she became excitedly aware of his body against her own and the sensation was like a huge bolt of electricity passing right through her. She took a shuddering breath as she felt his hard thighs move against her own. Her head was tilted back and their eyes met and united in a long, searching look before, tilting his own dark head, he closed the distance between their lips.

As she began to lose her hold on reality, she felt as if her entire body had been made for Karl and it was now in the process of becoming liberated. While his mouth continued to search hers, his hand moved to her breast, and sensations beyond belief swept through her and she found herself kissing him back with all the passion of a wanton gypsy girl.

There was just a trace of amusement in his grey eyes as he drew back to look at her—just enough to bring her to her senses.

As Karl released her he said, 'Chase those men up, Paula. If you don't, I will!'

With outraged eyes she watched him as he began to leave.

'Karl?' Her voice was very soft, but he heard.

He turned. 'Yes?'

'Don't you ever do that to me again. . .'

He crossed the room again. 'Don't you see what you are doing to yourself? You are all woman, and you are killing yourself—and what the hell for? I expected to see several stolid builders turn up here that day, and what happened? You turn up with these two ex-fishermen, but no matter how many men you employ this is still too much for you. This was not the agreement—not that I was aware of.'

'I'm not the first woman to be doing work like this, and I certainly won't be the last. Can't you see—the woman of today is. . .?'

'I am not concerned about the woman of today!'

he shouted. 'I am concerned only about you —
what is going on here. Forget about what other
women are doing! I'm not interested. Do you
understand?'

'No, I don't!' she shouted back.

For the next three weeks, Paula did her best to
keep out of Karl's way until she had no option but
to seek him out one day, to explain about the delay
on cement, which was now beginning to give rise
to concern and be the cause of not being able to go
on with much of the work.

She found him sorting out numerous and ancient
newspapers which had been stacked away in a
cupboard in the old-fashioned bathroom.

'*Yes*, Paula?' He did not look up and spoke with
impatience.

'Unfortunately, the cement I have on order
hasn't arrived. I haven't experienced this problem
before. I just can't understand it, but it should be
here any day now.'

'So you came here to tell me something I already
know for myself?' He lifted his dark lashes to look
at her. 'Well, Paula, I suppose a little wishful
thinking never hurt anyone. The cement could turn
up today, no? Or, if not today, then tomorrow — or
the next day — or the next. . .'

'Karl, why are you making things so impossible
for me?' she sighed. 'I can't talk to you any more.'

'I think, Paula, you are making things impossible

for yourself,' Karl said quietly. 'Look, there is nothing for it but to wait, no? Let's just wait for this cement. Why bother me with this?'

'Why indeed?' Her voice rose. 'With you, it's a case of look this and look that. I'm trying to get somewhere with you, Karl. Can't you understand that?'

He took a long breath and shoved the papers to one side. 'Put this delay to good use, instead of worrying about a situation which apparently cannot be avoided by your suppliers.'

'I am putting the delay to good use,' she told him. 'We're getting on with other jobs, after all, but I wanted you to know why it is that we seem to be fluctuating from one job to another.'

'Look, take time off, Paula. Get into something glamorous and get started on your book. You can write here, if you like — where it all started. I have a portable typewriter.'

The hint of sarcasm goaded her to fury. 'My book, Karl, is the last thing on my mind right now! I've got problems here, and I'm looking out for another suitable cottage. . .'

'Forget about the cottage. I told you, I'll sort something out. Close down the work until the cement arrives.' He was becoming angry again. 'This should please the ex-fishermen, no? Tell them to take a well-earned rest! After all, I see that Human Rights Day is just around the corner. Look, we'll go one better. We'll make it *several* Human

Rights Days. I'll close Sturmvögel and we will drive into the desert which probably claimed the life of your great-grandfather. How do you think you can be sensitive to the book if you don't do something about researching your background further by experiencing for yourself at least part of what lies beyond Lüderitz? It is to be your background, no?'

As she listened to him, Paula shook her head in amazement. 'I can't understand you. First you say, *Look* — you say, chase those men up. If you don't, I will. Then on the very next breath you say, We'll drive into the desert for a few days. Who exactly are we referring to here? What makes you think I'd go with you, anyway?'

'Let's cut the empty chatter, Paula, and talk about what I have just mentioned about driving into the desert. Between 1908 and 1914, some five million carats of diamonds were recovered from the desert. Since then, many more millions of carats have been found. There is a strong possibility that your great-grandfather, Rory Paul Stewart, left here to search for diamonds. He would have gone into the desert and, striking lucky, he would have gone on somewhere in an effort to sell them. Like him, you should get out there and experience the physical and emotional feelings of what it's like — to some extent, anyway. We have a hold-up here — let's put it to good use. It will only be for a few days.'

'Karl, this is a useless conversation. If Rory went

anywhere, it would have been to Kolmanskop, and I've been there. It's desert there! Let's face it, though, he probably cleared off with a fancy woman. He might have met her at the casino there. Perhaps she used to sing there — or even dance — you know, do the can-can, that sort of thing.'

'Your book will be *based* on your great-grand-father. When a man disappears the way he did, diamonds were probably at the back of everything.'

After a moment she said, 'Fine, but what you have in mind amounts to staying at campsites with nothing else but ablution blocks and refuse bins. . .places to make fires to cook — and I'm prudent enough not to want to share a tent or even a Land Rover with you at night.'

Karl laughed shortly, then crossed his arms as he leaned against the door. 'Although I function like any normal male — that is, with a strong desire for sexual gratification — I would not make you do anything you didn't want to do. As a matter of fact, Heinrich has come up with something. . .'

'Oh, come! What has Heinrich to do with all this?' demanded Paula. 'Although he had the key to Sturmvögel he kept that information from me — not that I would have expected him to open the castle without permission. He could have *told* me, though, that the castle was furnished — that sort of thing. Another thing: you make this driving into the desert, as you put it, sound so easy. We're not in Frankfurt, Karl. This isn't some convenient place tourists use as a base for excursions to neighbouring cities and towns. This is a desert we're talking about. What you're suggesting is madness!'

'Horst must have been mad to have built this damned castle in the first place,' said Karl. 'It is certainly giving me many headaches! In fact, I've just remembered. . .he wrote along these lines. . . "My madness has paid off. By the grace of God, we have built the Castle Sturmvögel." What is more, Paula, *your* great-grandfather must have been mad to have come here from Ireland, not knowing what to expect, huh? So why not throw in a little more madness?'

Forgetting her hostility for a moment, Paula said, 'My thoughts often go to Hannah, who must have been here while the castle was being built. I wonder where she stayed?'

'According to records we have in the family, in Lüderitz. After all, the diamond rush was on, no? This gave rise to an affluent community. Tell me, are you afraid I'll get us lost?' His grey eyes were suddenly mocking.

'Up to a point.' She gave him a level look.

'What does that mean?' His eyes held hers.

'It means I don't like you. You have the ability to unsettle me. It means that you've overstepped the mark with me.'

'I give you my word, you'll be perfectly safe with me,' said Karl. 'Tell me, Paula, is it me you don't trust?' he mocked, 'or yourself?'

CHAPTER FOUR

AFTER weeks of sheer frustration and hard work, Paula was feeling bone tired, and the very last thing she felt like was having to cope without Kobus and Johnny, who were to attend a funeral and would not be working at Sturmvögel.

When Karl spoke from behind her, she deliberately sighed.

'Where are the men today?' There was a degree of annoyance in his voice.

'They've gone to a funeral,' she answered shortly, then continued to hammer at a wall which was now earmarked to accommodate a long window, instead of the existing embrasure.

'A funeral?' Karl queried.

Resenting the aggression in his voice, she said, 'That's what I said, Karl—a funeral. They won't be working today.'

'How do you work that one out? A funeral does not take all day, surely?'

'Why are you so unfeeling? This is a funeral we're talking about!' Paula could feel her temper rising.

'I am not unfeeling. I am curious.' He continued to subject her to that steel-grey look which always

79

made her think of a storm about to break over the Atlantic Ocean.

'A funeral *can* take all day. For one thing, there's a wake next to none. There will be saxophones and banjos — food, drink. . .'

'And so once again, in that case, you will be here all day on your own? It was only last week that there was a wedding, no? With a reception next to none.'

'Karl, I'm waiting to get on here, if you don't mind.' Paula sighed pointedly.

'Why don't you concentrate on something else? Leave that wall for those individuals, when they decide to come back.' Karl's impatience and aggression had given way to anger. 'This is not the sort of work you should be doing. Have you taken leave of your senses?'

'Oh, let's not go into this again, Karl, *please!*'

'I have had enough of this. Leave that wall. I am giving you an order, Paula!'

Moving with a leopard's sense of timing, he reached for the heavy hammer she was holding, and she caught her breath in surprise, then watched him furiously as he flung it to the floor.

After a moment of stunned silence she said in a cold voice, 'Kindly pick that hammer up, Karl, and pass it to me.'

At that moment his grey eyes were like hard, polished metal and her heart was beginning to race, for she had never seen him so angry.

She watched him as he picked up the hammer, but, instead of handing it to her, he began to leave with it.

Turning to look at her, he said, 'I can no longer tolerate this madness. I am up to here.' He drew a finger of his free hand across his throat. 'I cannot support it, and I absolutely forbid you, Paula, to use this weapon again. Do you understand?'

'No, I don't understand! Far from it, in fact. How dare you carry on like this? You're being unreasonable. You are, in fact, interfering with the way in which I earn my living!' she snapped.

'Why don't you have the common sense to choose to earn it some other way?' he asked.

'What was I expected to do, when it came to the point when I had to start thinking of a way to earn money? Beg? Borrow? Steal?' As she spoke, Paula kept telling herself that this couldn't be happening—not again! 'It's got nothing to do with you!'

'It has everything to do with me, since I am now very much involved. If you found yourself in financial difficulties. . .'

'Not *if*,' she interrupted, '*when* I found myself in financial difficulties.'

'OK—*when*!' Karl's voice rose. 'When you found yourself in financial difficulties you did not have to beg, borrow or steal. Why, for instance, did you not think about approaching the office of the Karakul weavery, or the museum? You never cease to amaze me.' He made a baffled gesture.

After he had gone, taking the hammer — weapon, as he had called it — with him, tears of anger and frustration stung Paula's eyes, while depression began to claw at her like a bird of prey.

She spent the rest of the day sandpapering a panelled wall which had to be treated, and as she worked, her mind flounced from one unsettling subject to another. She thought about her wishy-washy and selfish relationship with Josh, where she enjoyed his advances — but only up to a point. She brooded about money matters and the way in which she had gone about earning money to get herself back home, without having to harass her already worried father. Why, she asked herself, had she gone on staying in Lüderitz? The answer had nothing to do with its unique situation between the endless expanse of the Namib's monotonous coastline, weatherbeaten rocks or the pounding of the Atlantic. Why then had she stayed on after she had finished researching Lüderitz and Kolmanskop, the sand-smothered and deserted diamond-mining settlement which might have played a role in Rory Stewart's life? Surrounded by the sands of the desert, Kolmanskop must surely have beckoned to him as he considered the glitter of diamonds which might have come his way. Surely she had had a good foundation for the book she intended writing, without staying on?

* * *

Windhoek would have offered more scope when it came to finding a job. Shopping facilities were excellent, after all, and Paula could have found work in a jeweller's shop. There were countless shops dealing in diamonds and magnificent semi-precious gemstones and mineral specimens, not to mention curio shops which sold handcarved wooden objects and dolls dressed in the traditional Herero style and made by Herero women. She had, Paula thought dismally, opted for the hard way, and, what was more, had even hoped to get permission, one day, to restore at least one of the sand-blasted buildings in Kolmanskop.

At the back of everything, of course, had been the castle. As she thought about it now, she realised that her sixth sense must have told her that she would eventually find herself on the inside of these thick sandstone walls. If, then, she'd *had* to be near Sturmvögel, to brood on her book, why hadn't she done something like starting her own safari outfit and called it Paula's Safaris? Josh could have designed the colourful brochure. . . Experience the *real* Africa with Paula and her team. . .

'Paula!'

At the sound of Karl's voice she jumped and then looked at him with resentful eyes.

Karl's handsome face was expressionless. 'To use a term popular with your ex-fishermen, it is time to knock off!'

After a moment she said, 'I'll decide when it's

time to knock off, Karl.' She gave him a cold stare, then glanced at her watch. A whole working day had slipped by, she thought, and she had not stopped once — and it felt like it!

'This is one time, Paula, when you don't decide. Do I have to spell it out for you? You have not stopped the entire day!'

'No, you don't have to remind me. It might satisfy you to know that it *feels* as if I've not stopped the entire day, actually.'

He came over to her and took the sandpaper, which was wrapped around a thick wedge of wood, away from her and threw it against the stone wall opposite.

'And so, in other words, you are dead beat? You are craving to relax? Tell me, what happens when you get home every day? Do you get a chance to relax?' He looked at her with a degree of concern. 'Or do you go on driving yourself there too?'

'Mostly, again for your satisfaction, I collapse — which is, I suppose, the nearest thing to relaxing. Is that what you want to hear?' Her voice was edgy and tense.

'What had you planned to do tonight, for instance?'

'Collapse. What else? For about half an hour. Then take a bath and change and take time off to eat, followed by bed. Every woman fantasises about the sheer luxury of being pampered or, at least, pampering herself, but this is the most I can come up with at the present time.'

'Well, tonight there will be a change of routine. You won't have to fantasise, for you will spend the night here and I will see to it that you relax, not just collapse.'

Paula was momentarily confused. 'What are you talking about?'

'Tonight I have a surprise in store for you. In a few moments, however, you will start by getting out of those repugnant clothes and relaxing in a bath, after which I will have a drink waiting for you, followed by a crayfish supper. In other words, I intend to remind you, first, that you are a woman in need of pampering.'

Paula could not believe what she was hearing. 'What? Am I going mad or something? Or have you taken leave of your senses?' She was aware that she had begun to shake and made to get past him, but he caught her by the shoulders.

'Let go of me, Karl.' Somehow she managed to keep her voice quiet and controlled. 'I have to get home, and you know how bad the road is. I'm not in possession of some fancy Land Rover 110 to get me over it. There might even be a sandstorm, and here you are, holding me up. I want to go home, if you don't mind!'

'What you want and what is going to happen instead are two different things. Make up your mind to it, Paula, you are not going home.'

'What are you getting at? Are you calmly telling me that you intend forcing me to stay here for the night? What's more, do you honestly expect me to get undressed here, step into a bath and then relax over a drink? This, you say, will be followed by a crayfish supper, no less.' Her eyes were full of shocked indignation. 'You must be joking, surely?'

'I'm not joking, and unless I have to, I do not intend to force you to do these things. You will do them of your own accord.'

Their eyes locked and clung, and Paula felt her legs almost give way.

'You wouldn't dare force me! I don't need this in my life, Karl!'

When she tried again to get past him he caught her to him and held her close. Panic fluttered inside her and she immediately began to fight him.

Very softly he asked, 'Do you want *me* to undress you?'

'Just you try!' Her voice rose. 'Let go of me!'

'I have had enough of seeing you slaving here every day,' he told her savagely, 'looking blind with tiredness at the end of it.' He held her tightly within the circle of one arm and began to undo the buttons of her denim shirt, stopping only to ask, 'Is this what you want? Do you want me to continue, or will you go to the bathroom and do it yourself?'

At this moment, Paula thought desperately, Karl had merciless eyes.

'Keep your hands to yourself, Karl!' Aware of the sudden desire in his grey eyes, she shouted, 'You'll answer for this, I promise you!'

Without paying the slightest attention to what she was saying, Karl continued to look her over before he released her.

'Do you realise how beautiful you are? Why do you do these things to yourself? You're something like the flora of this country, Paula, do you know that? You persist in clinging to hard desert conditions. Paula, within the next hour, I want to see you relaxed and serene — the way you should be. I have had enough of seeing you like this.'

'You want to see me relaxed and serene? How do you expect me to feel serene, calm and tranquil? I have no intention of staying here. You must be as mad as that great-grandfather of yours!' When she tried to get at Karl's face with her nails, he stunned her by lifting her into his arms.

Shutting her mind to everything now, she realised that she was going to have to outsmart him, and escape. She felt herself shaking, but forced herself to keep calm. Once she was alone in the bathroom, she reasoned, she would get away from the castle as quickly as possible.

By this time Karl had carried her through to the bathroom and she began to struggle again.

'Leave me! If I *have* to bath, I'm capable of getting into the water by myself.'

'Calm down, Paula. Damn it, do you want us

both to break our backs? I am trying to convince
you that all I want is for you to soak the tiredness
from your body and to make you see some sense.
You cannot go on like this, day after day. You will
kill youself!'

'I'll scream this place down in a minute, Karl!'

'What good do you think that will do you, huh?
It would appear that I will have to force you. Is
that what you want?'

As they struggled together, Paula felt herself
slipping and grabbed on to the side of the bath and
tried to pull herself up, but, regardless of the fact
that she was still fully clothed, Karl managed to get
her into the water, and when she gave up in
despair, he straightened and looked down at her.
The fact that he was sopping wet gave her a certain
amount of satisfaction.

'I wish you'd broken your neck, you asp! Do you
consider this kind of behaviour to be the privilege
of the *rich*? The privilege of a *count*?' Her shock and
fright were giving way to wild fury, and, feeling
nearly sick, as a result she screamed, 'Get out! Just
get out of here, before I do something we'll both
regret!'

After he had gone, she covered her face with her
hands while desolation swept over her.

Karl returned almost immediately and tossed a
flowing garment over the chair. 'I will have a drink
waiting for you in the library when you are finished
here. Take your time.'

'If you think I'm putting that on, you have another think coming! How many women have had to wear it in these hideous circumstances, I wonder?'

'Believe it or not—none. I had purchased this Herero dress in Windhoek for my beautiful and apparently ageless mother, but since I have not got round to sending it off to her. . .'

'There's no need to deprive your beautiful and apparently ageless mother. Take it away!' Paula looked up at him with hostile blue eyes.

'Don't be foolish! Your clothes are already wet. Put that dress on, Paula. I can assure you, you will be the first to wear it—and the last!'

'Get out of my sight!' she shouted. 'I'm totally disgusted with you!'

'Well, maybe that cuts two ways, Paula. Maybe I am disgusted with you also. What have you been trying to turn yourself into? Some freak?'

As he turned to leave she shouted, 'You can get someone else to finish the repairs to your miserable castle!'

The moment he left, she took off her wet clothes and flung them with all her strength across the room, then wondered what to do. Karl had left her feeling totally shattered.

Finally she went over to the door and turned the key in the old-fashioned lock. Getting back into the water, she began to soap herself, while she tried to sort things out in her mind.

After a few moments she calmed down and got out of the antiquated bath, with its wooden surround, and began to dry herself with one of the bold-coloured towels Karl had obviously bought in Windhoek.

Because she had no option, she picked up the Herero dress, which was really very beautiful, and she could see why Karl had bought it for his mother. The various Herero tribes, she knew, took pride in their clothes, and women of the major Herero group from the country's central region adapted their style from the Victorian fashions worn by the early missionaries' wives.

This particular dress was high-waisted and as full as a caftan. It also had long, wide sleeves and was made of showy cotton material which had big squares in colours of pale blue, cobalt blue, white, red, pumpkin and vivid green. Each square was outlined in dark brown. Paula knew that a Herero woman would match this dress with a shawl, either knitted or of a different shade of material — or even of lace.

Once the garment was on, she had to turn back the sleeves, which were too long for her, and the result was nothing short of stylish.

Using the cream Karl had left out for her, she creamed her face and then, unlocking the door, she made for the room in which she had been working before Karl had arrived to infuriate and humiliate her.

Her bag, along with the keys to her cottage and pick-up, was gone.

From behind her Karl said softly, 'I have them, Paula. What else did you expect?'

'I want my keys, Karl.' Stay cool, she warned herself. 'Since I have had no option but to wear this dress, I'll let you have a cheque for it. You'd better find someone else to finish the work here. You were right—this is a bad idea.' She held out her hand which, she noticed, trembled slightly. 'My keys—or are you deaf?'

He looked at her with cool assessment and she saw the admiration in his eyes. 'You will have your keys tomorrow, when you need them. You know, looking at you, Paula, I have never wanted a woman so much.'

She felt her heartbeat quicken. What was he planning? Was he hoping to seduce her? For he must have known all this time that in spite of everything she was attracted to him. Of all the men she had to go and fall in love with—for she fully realised she was in love with him—it had to be a man who thought nothing of displaying his arrogance and the scorn he felt towards her.

'In that case,' she made for the door, 'I'll walk back to Lüderitz.'

Karl stepped in front of her. 'How long do you think it would take you to cover that rough road in your bare feet, huh?' He smiled faintly. 'Be reasonable.'

'Reasonable?' she echoed. 'You're the one who's not being reasonable. You can't keep me here against my will. There's a law against this sort of thing. You're an educated person, you should know that!'

She watched him as he shrugged carelessly. 'Oh, I agree. I am quite aware of the fact, believe me. You don't even have to be very well educated to know that!'

'In that case, let me out of here. Be aware of one thing—if you *don't*, Karl, I intend going straight to the police. I'll have you hunted out of Lüderitz!'

'Like George Pond of London, in fact?' His eyes mocked her for a moment before he became serious. 'Things got out of control. I'm sorry for what happened—you've got to believe that!'

'You're not sorry. You don't know *how* to be sorry!' she snapped furiously.

'That's not true. You seem to forget that you misled me from the word go. I have been carrying this anger, Paula, around with me from the time you turned up here with that cement-mixer, dressed like a man, ready for manual work.'

'I'm not interested in your excuses.' She dragged her fingers through her damp auburn hair. 'This whole thing is as bizarre as many of the plants which appear in the desert—and that goes for the crystal rosette known as the desert rose, as well. Just let me out of here. I warn you, Karl, you'll be sorry you ever met me!'

When he reached for her hand, she snatched it away. 'Don't you dare touch me again!'

'Come, Paula, don't prolong this.' His eyes searched her face. 'We discussed fate once. Put everything that has happened to you down to the fate of being beautiful.'

'I've told you, I'm waiting for my keys. I'm not coming!'

'If you don't come willingly, I will have to carry you, in that case,' he said calmly.

Paula caught her breath and then began to fight him as, like some 1920s hero, he lifted her up and carried her to the library.

As soon as he put her down, and as shocked and outraged as she was, she was amazed at the transformation which had taken place in the library since she had last had occasion to enter it.

Lamps and candles were burning everywhere. A fire crackled in the huge fireplace. Somewhere along the line, Karl must have got Cecil Peters to help him move a simple sleigh bed from one of the smaller bedrooms and, backed by large pink and crimson cushions, it now resembled an elegant sofa.

Karl was saying, 'A woman in Lüderitz made the cushions only this morning—what you might call a rush job. While you were working, I drove into Lüderitz to collect the food which I had ordered yesterday. You see, since I have a surprise in store for you, I had planned something like this—that we should dine at the castle tonight.'

'So you went to Lüderitz and you didn't even have the decency to tell me—so that I could lock myself in? It's very lonely here. Have you no consideration for people, Karl?'

'Knowing full well that you would not break the whole day, I took the necessary precaution of locking you in. It shows I have good judgement. You *didn't* stop. Besides, I was not gone for long.'

They stared into each other's eyes. 'And so you had all this planned? *Right from yesterday*?' Paula began to tremble again.

'Only up to a point. Things, after all, got out of control. You see, I had intended to speak to you this morning about making arrangements to pick you up after you had dropped your men off and had time to go home and change. I fully intended, Paula, to drive you back after we had eaten here, but when I saw you standing there, covered in dust from sandpapering that large expanse of panelling and looking blurred with exhaustion, I had a brainstorm. Things got out of hand. I guess I wanted to punish you for what you are doing to yourself.'

'You said you intended to pick me up and then take me back home, after we'd eaten here, but the fact that I was alone here, without my ex-fishermen to protect me, proved too much of a temptation to you, is that it? I was alone and completely at your mercy.' Paula spoke in a soft, vulnerable voice.

'Your being at my mercy, Paula, never entered my mind. What do you take me for? I repeat, what took place here was the result of a brainstorm on my part. Sometimes you look blind with fatigue. It maddens me to see it!'

'What you succeeded in doing, Karl, was to leave me feeling like some wounded, stricken creature. That's exactly how I feel,' she told him bitterly.

'You know, I don't know which is worse,' he spoke with unusual gentleness, 'seeing you look a mess and covered in dust, or beautiful with your lovely face strangled with unhappiness. Paula. . .' he came towards her '. . .I'm sorry. Forgive me.'

The atmosphere was rigid with tension. For a moment their eyes held together and, in spite of everything which had happened, a shock of excitement raced through her.

'I'm sorry,' Karl said again. 'I've just asked you to forgive me.'

'Do try to understand if I fail—dismally.' Her voice was brittle with hurt and sarcasm. 'I find it impossible to forgive you.'

She heard him sigh before he went to the drinks table and then he came back to her with a glass of wine.

'I don't want wine!' snapped Paula. 'I want to leave. I'm going to dinner with Josh, and he'll be looking for me.'

'In that case, Josh is in for a disappointment, no? Take this, Paula!' Karl's voice had hardened. 'It will do you good.'

She drew a deep breath and kept her eyes on his face as she took the glass from him.

'By the way,' his tone was slightly mocking now, 'since I could not buy flowers, I decided to do the next best thing.'

Paula realised that he was referring to the large number of semi-precious stones and raw minerals which were piled into round, shallow baskets. More were displayed on the desk and side-tables. It was a beautiful sight of blue-lace agate, amethyst, rose-quartz and tourmaline, ranging from pink to green and blue. Two large and carefully glazed ceramic pitchers, in shades of pink and blue, stood on the floor, and attached to their handles were ceramic beads which had been strung on to thick cord. The flagged floor was partly covered by a new cream Karakul rug which felt snug against her feet.

Karl raised his glass. 'Maybe the time is ripe to drink to your book?'

'I'm here against my will, Karl, and you expect me to drink with you, just as though nothing has happened? And yet all this is the result of careful planning on your part.'

'Along with the surprise I have in store for you, yes, and which I believe will play a part in this book. I suggest you have something to eat. Try one of these canapés.'

While he was speaking, Paula took a small sip of her wine and tried to scheme how she could escape. She crossed over to the table with the canapés and took one of them, then lifted her lashes to look at Karl in his white cotton trousers and black polo-necked sweater. He was again wholly in command, she thought bitterly, attractive and frightening. His brainstorm, as he had called it, had thrown him only temporarily. What gentleness and concern there had been a little while ago were gone.

'I'm going out with Josh tonight—I've told you that. We'd planned to eat at Otto's Seafood, and Josh will be expecting me to be at my cottage when he calls for me.'

'Well, sometimes the best plans have a habit of backfiring—and, Paula, you know that I speak from personal experience—so forget about Josh. What I have in mind tonight is more important than the artist.'

As she listened to him, Paula found herself wondering where Karl had managed to buy such huge logs in an area where there were no forests—but then, she mused bitterly, he was capable of anything, even buying logs in a desert area.

She glanced down at her glass, which had been polished until it glittered. On Karl's instructions, Cecil Peters had obviously been busy in more ways

than one. The glass was, of course, an heirloom
which, for a short time anyway, had found its way
back into the family again, along with everything
else in the castle. She also wondered whether Karl
would have any of the treasures shipped back to
Germany before he left Namibia and, once he was
back home, would forget about tonight, or at the
most, look back on it with amusement.

Her long sigh was plainly audible over the crack-
ling of the burning logs.

He broke into these thoughts. 'What are you
thinking about?'

'Karl, you *must* know how I used to drive out
here and sit and look up at this castle and long to
get inside it?' Her voice was soft. 'Little did I know
that I'd find myself a prisoner in it—but then you
did hint at the possibility when you mentioned a
secret chamber, after all.'

'You are allowing your vivid imagination to run
away with you. You are anything but a prisoner.
You will be free to do as you like tomorrow. You
know that!'

'Sometimes,' she went on, 'Sturmvögel appeared
so stark and cruel—like you, in fact.' She put her
glass down. 'Why am I holding this? I don't want
it. I don't want anything from you—not even the
contract, any more.'

'If you don't want your wine, we will go through
to the dining-room, and since Otto prepared everything, you will still be enjoying his food. There

was, after all, no need for Josh to take you to Otto's restaurant.'

'I can't seems to get through to you,' she sighed. 'I don't want to eat! The way I feel right now, food would choke me!'

'In that case, since we don't want you to choke,' Karl said brutally, 'you will watch *me* eat. Are you going to walk this time, or shall I. . .?'

'What do you think?' she cut in angrily. 'Apparently I have no option, since I can't bear the thought of you touching me.'

The dining-room was lit by many candles which burned in pewter sconces, and there were tall candlesticks on the long table. Paula's eyes went to the food set out on the sideboard and she suddenly realised just how empty she was feeling, for she had not eaten since six in the morning. . .not hungry, but just empty and miserable. Everything looked cool and inviting, and it was obvious that Karl had used cool-bags to keep it that way. A wind had got up, and even though the sandstone walls were thick, it could be heard surging round the lonely and isolated castle.

'To put your mind at rest, Paula, I have no intention of forcing you to submit—unwillingly, that is—to any advances I might be tempted to make towards you tonight,' Karl told her. 'I suggest, therefore, that you try to enjoy your food—

without choking, that is. Later, if you still insist, I will drive you back to Lüderitz.'

Her shattered spirits lifted immediately. 'Is that a promise?'

'I cannot give you that assurance. A promise is not something I give or take lightly. Who knows? By the sound of what is going on outside, there could even be a sandstorm.'

'And that's exactly why you made this promise, isn't it?' Her tone was full of bitterness.

'And you jump to too many conclusions,' he told her curtly.

Hoping to get this experience behind her, Paula decided to do as he suggested by going to the sideboard and helping herself to crayfish and salads. Going back to the table, she sat down opposite him at the one end of the long, gleaming table.

Karl poured wine into tall, pink-stemmed wine-glasses. The candles on the table burned between them and highlighted his handsome face and intensified his grey eyes.

Lifting those eyes to hers, he said, 'Since you have no wish to drink to your book, I suggest we drink to the bloom of the grape.'

For a moment she stared back at him. 'I have to hand it to you, Count von Buren, I'm amazed at just how organised you are at Sturmvögel. Everything is gleaming and glittering. Obviously, at your persuasive instructions, Cecil Peters has been busy.'

'That is exactly what I am paying him for, after all.' Karl's eyes were direct.

'Logs in the vast fireplace and all—but then, as you have yourself admitted, you are a proficient shopper. Where did you go for the logs? Canada?' Paula gave Karl a spiteful look.

'I have *had* to be a proficient shopper since arriving in Namibia. I am, after all, on a survival beat,' he mocked. 'Something like you, in fact.'

'Oh, not quite, since, with you, *money* is at the back of your survival beat,' she retorted.

'Well, it happens to be at the back of everything with you too, no?' He smiled faintly.

'Yes, that's true. The lack of it. Tell me, how come you were unable to come up with several huge bouquets?' Her voice was stiff with sarcasm.

He shrugged. 'There was no time to have flowers flown in from Holland—not even for you. What I have arranged instead will have to suffice. Another time, perhaps. You will have to enlighten me as to your taste in flowers.'

'This isn't a game, Karl. Since there won't be a next time, flowers won't be necessary.'

'No? Don't be too sure. Apart from the logs, of course, all the gleam and glitter was here, just waiting to be revived. I have explained how this castle has changed hands several times, and always with most of its contents. Most of what is here— furniture, works of art, porcelain and so on—goes back to Horst's day.'

'And for years Herr Heinrich has been looking after it all but didn't have the courtesy to tell me.' Paula could not keep the hostility from her voice. 'I always thought the castle was empty.'

Karl leaned back in his chair and surveyed her critically. 'Wars, Paula, leaves their scars on people. Heinrich was interned during World War Two — just as my father would have been interned if he'd happened to have been out here at that particular time. As a result of what happened to him, Heinrich grew into the habit of keeping his mouth shut. It would have been completely out of character if he had told you about the keys.'

The wine was richly fragrant and must have cost a small fortune, Paula thought, as she took a sip. As hungry as she found herself to be, she was only able to pick at her food. The dessert had also been prepared by Otto, and as she ate it, she tilted her head back so that she could gaze at the heavily beamed ceiling.

Karl's eyes followed her own as he held his glass with his fingertips and sat back in that arrogant, elegant way of his.

'Rory Paul Stewart probably worked on those mammoth beams. You realise that, of course? I had always planned for you to see them by candlelight like this. I suggest, since this party is very much in his honour, tonight, we drink to him.' He raised his glass. 'To Rory Paul.'

Quite suddenly Paula felt like breaking down. Karl had spoilt a wonderful moment for her.

When she had herself under control she said, 'In very different circumstances, Karl, this would have meant so much to me. Why did you have to go about it in such a disgusting manner? I can hardly credit that you expect me to sit here as though nothing has happened, and yet everything was cunningly contrived by you, which just goes to show how callous you are.'

'I am not as callous as you think. Anyway, here's to your great-grandfather, Paula. Let us drink to him before I show you something interesting presently.'

She tried not to show interest, but she was, in fact, beginning to ask herself what all this was about.

After a moment she lifted her glass. 'In that case, to my great-grandfather—and yours.' Her voice was low and bitter. 'Thanks to both of them, we're both here tonight.'

CHAPTER FIVE

'I HAVE discovered the secret door which was referred to by Horst in his diaries,' said Karl, when they were back in the library. 'Although he made reference to this door and how to go about opening it, he did not reveal its position. You won't believe this, but I have spent nights on end tapping panelling.' His laugh was soft and mocking. 'I think I must have covered every inch, but it has paid off. At last I have found the door which, in turn, leads to a door to the secret room. This room, by the way, was to be used by the family in a possible crisis.'

Paula found herself staring at his well-shaped hands, which were tanned and strong, and felt a shudder pass right through her.

'If this is the surprise, Karl, I don't really think I want to see this secret room,' she told him. 'What's more, I don't think you're being fair. You said you'd drive me home after we'd eaten.'

'Why don't you wait and see what all this is about?' he snapped. 'You are always one leap ahead.' He placed the torch which he had taken from a drawer in the desk and put it on a side-table near the wall. He then began to manoeuvre a section of the panelling which swung back from the wall on completely concealed hinges. 'It is so skilfully invented that, during those periods when the castle changed hands, it is apparent that no one ever got to find out about it, as it is not even mentioned in later records of the history of Sturmvögel.' He stood back and reached for the torch. 'If you come over here, you will see the second door.'

When Paula made no move, he turned to look at her. 'What is it? This is of particular interest to *you*.' He showed his annoyance.

Paula's nerves were on edge, but after a moment she joined him. 'What is it? Let's get this over so that I can go home, Karl.'

'See what is carved into the wood here. It is so finely done as to be almost overlooked.'

As her eyes became used to the torchlight they flew at once to the words 'Rory Paul Stewart', which were carved beneath what, after she had read it, appeared to be a proverb.

The words were small and beautifully carved, and in a low voice she began to read. 'But whoso committeth adultery with a woman lacketh understanding: he that doth it destroyeth his own soul. Rory Paul Stewart.'

'Oh, no!' In the stillness of the confined space she looked at Karl. 'You know what this means, don't you? He obviously committed adultery. This, then, was the reason he never went back to my great-grandmother—he met another woman and had an affair with her. Two things could have happened—after he got around to kicking and loathing himself—he just disappeared, or else he cleared off with *her*.'

'What man, Paula, doesn't have a fling from time to time? Men have always had a reputation for enjoying a spell of indulgence.' Karl spoke with exasperation.

'That's exactly the way you *would* look at things!' she flared. 'You are, after all, no better than he was. I feel absolutely deflated. I'd built him up in my mind until he became some sort of hero. Why did you have to show me this?'

'You are so quick to condemn. Do you expect that he should have lived the life of a celibate while he was out here?'

'Well, if he had to have a woman, why didn't he face up to the fact that he was a man with a wife and two children waiting for him in Ireland and go back to them eventually when his little fling was over? What is it you called it? After he'd enjoyed his *spell of indulgence*!'

'There must have been another reason why he didn't go back home after the affair was over. Maybe after he got round to kicking and loathing himself, as *you* put it, he decided to leave here, to hide his face, and decided—like you—to earn a living by doing something stupid. Maybe, on the other hand, he was sick of working here because he didn't get on with Horst. Who knows? Maybe he just wanted some adventure in his life.'

'Something stupid — like what?' asked Paula

'Like dealing in illicit diamonds. Who is to tell? Maybe, as a result of this craving for adventure, he *did* get himself lost in the desert, for that is what you have always believed, no?'

Paula moved back into the centre of the library. 'Like you,' she said, with considerable malice, 'he was just a typical man! You know, Karl, I'd made up my mind that I'd be going back to Ireland without ever having the chance of getting to see inside this castle, let alone working here and then being shown something like this.'

'That was before fate stepped in.' Karl closed the secret door. 'It was my appointed lot in life to come and find you in Namibia.'

'And my appointed lot to be outraged by you! The point is, why did you have to go about showing me this writing on the panel by violating me first? You're no better than he was. Like you, he couldn't keep his hands off women, apparently.'

'The point is, Paula, it's not me we're talking about here,' said Karl. 'We are talking about *him*. Maybe, as I have just pointed out, he did decide to leave this woman. After all, it was the very height of the diamond mania. Maybe he had grand ideas of returning to Ireland with a pouch full of diamonds. What about this place — Kolmanskop? This settlement, as you have already pointed out, might have played a part in his life. You talk about being violated, however. To violate means to have outraged you — to have raped you, in other words. Were you raped by me?' His voice was alarmingly soft, and even in the subdued lighting, she felt the power of his steel-grey eyes.

'You kept me here against my will. You manhandled me! Isn't that a violation? Let me tell you something: from a woman's point of view, *it is*!' She shouted the last two words at him. 'Believe me, so far as a woman is concerned, that was nothing else but violation!'

'One thing led to another. I lost my head and I stand rebuked,' he retorted with an anger that matched her own.

'Is that all you have to say? "I lost my head"? It was a calculated insult! What I can't understand is why you had to do the things you did to me. Why didn't you just come to me and tell me that you had something of interest to show me concerning my great-grandfather?' She lifted her shoulders and spread her hands. 'OK, you could have asked me to have supper here. I'd have enjoyed that, actually. I would have gone home, first, to change, and *what is more*, I would have bathed. Did you think for one moment that the only way I'd ever get into a bathroom was by being physically manhandled there? I can't believe that actually happened. I just don't understand you.'

'Don't try to understand,' he told her. 'The fact is, I lost my head. I wanted to tear those workman's clothes off you and remind you that you have the face, the eyes, the hair and the body of a desirable and lovely woman. You seem to have forgotten that.'

'I'm quite aware of my body. I'm in contact with it every day, actually. The person you wanted to remind was yourself! I don't need some wealthy count to come out from Bavaria to remind me that I have one.'

'Am I to believe your artist does it for you? Does *he* remind you?'

'Is that what worries you? That he might have access to it and you don't?' She spoke with difficulty.

'It worries me, yes. Look, Paula, I have never done anything like this, before — not to any woman.' Karl smiled faintly.

'This isn't a joking matter. So it was a unique experience for you? How nice for you! It should become quite a drinking-out-with-the-boys story when you get back home. Guys, there was this girl in Namibia and boy, was she something!'

'My tastes do not revolve around club or locker-room talk with the boys, Paula. I have confessed, have I not, that I started out to shock you — to wake you up to the fact that you are not some kind of workman?' He sighed. 'I have never known a girl like you for creating problems. Well, perhaps I have — but that is beside the point right now.'

'Did you expect me not to fight back? Why have you made things so impossible for me? At the moment, I'm powerless to change my lifestyle. I *have* to go on working here, when I come to think of it. Everything has been ordered for the changes here. A lot is still on order. This is a castle we're restoring, after all, not some small rose-smothered cottage at the end of an English country lane. I can't just drop this project now, no matter how many times I've threatened to.' Paula put a hand over her eyes.

Suddenly she completely broke down. This is what he wants, she thought.

When he reached for her, she tried to scratch his face, but he caught her wrists and held them. Her tear-blinded eyes met his.

'Paula, don't!' His voice was very soft. 'I think, deep down, you know the position. I am in love with you. I don't want to see you slogging here every day.'

'Oh, sure! You're in love with me!' she snapped.

'It happens to be the truth.' He released her wrists and drew her to him, and she was immediately conscious of his strength and the sensation of intense longing that spread through her as he moulded her against his body and sought her lips.

When he kissed her, it was with extreme gentleness. She'd had no idea he could be so gentle, she thought.

'Ah, Paula. . .' His voice was muffled against her lips and then he drew away to look at her. 'What have you done to me, huh? Just what is going on here? I did not come to Namibia for the impossible to happen—to meet a girl I want more than any other girl I have ever met—but it has happened. I have, and in so many ways she causes me much concern. This isn't a game with me. I love you. Look at me. . .' He put his fingers beneath her chin.

As his lips sought hers again, he lifted her up and carried her to the sleigh bed which had been disguised as a sofa, and after he had put her down, Paula's eyes followed him as he lowered himself beside her.

'My darling,' he whispered, 'I want you, so much. . .'

'I don't know why it's had to come about this way, Karl,' she sighed, 'but I love you too. I want *you*—so very much.'

His hands began to explore her body, and Paula felt weak with the longing she was feeling to have him make love to her completely.

She was not sure at what moment they both became aware of the sound of the motor horn outside the castle. It sounded as if it had jammed.

Beginning to feel flustered and stupid now, as the desire she had been feeling began to climb down, she said, 'Is that my pick-up? The hooter seems to have jammed, Karl!'

'Forget it.' His voice contained irritation. 'I'll attend to it later. Who is here but us, after all? Paula, come here! There is no one for it to disturb. We are quite alone!'

She tried to fight her way back to the excitement she had been feeling and to concentrate on the marvellous things he was doing to her body, but the sound of the hooter had changed. She listened and began to count—three short, one long, three short, one long. . .

It's not my pick-up at all, she thought wildly. It's coming from Josh's car!

'Karl,' she tried to wriggle free of him, 'I know that hooter—it's coming from Josh's car. I *told* you we were going out to dinner. Obviously he's come to look for me and he's seen my pick-up outside.'

Karl drew back angrily. 'If he does not exist for you in that way, let him hoot. What is it with you? Does what was about to happen here between us lie in his decision to turn up here at the wrong moment?'

'Karl, no!' she protested. 'Please try to understand. I've lost all interest. I can't help it—I'm sorry.'

'You have lost all interest? Well, I haven't.' He pulled her to him and kissed her.

'Karl, I can't handle this. I'm sorry—honestly. Women aren't like men—surely you know that? The least thing switches them off.'

'And in this case, the least thing happens to be this drop-out artist who turns up looking for you. Why? Because he means something to you? Well, go to him, Paula, if that is what you want!'

'That's not fair, Karl! You keep calling Josh a drop-out. He's not a drop-out. He happens to be a serious artist, but a bit eccentric, that's all.'

Karl twisted himself and stood up. 'In that case, go to him. Maybe you will end up finishing what has started here at your cottage—if you can wait that long!'

'That's a terrible thing to say!' she sniffed angrily. 'How can you say that when you have just told me you love me, Karl? What's more, I told you how I feel about you.'

He looked down at her. 'Forget it. I'm beginning to get the picture.'

'Don't hurt me,' she said quietly. 'Damn it, I've been hurt enough.'

'In that case, why don't you let him clear off? Tell me, what has it got to do with him if you choose to spend the night with me?'

'I didn't exactly *choose* to spend the night here, did I? But in any case Josh has obviously been worried about me. You know what that road is like. You also know we get sandstorms—mostly outside Lüderitz, it's true, but by the sounds of it, there might even be one going on right now. Listen to the wind! I must have my keys—the keys to my cottage and the keys to my pick-up are together.'

The big studded door was unlocked by the time Paula got to it, but there was no sign of Karl. He had almost thrown her jeans, wet shirt and keys at her and then, apparently, gone to unlock and open the door for her.

Wind tore at the long Herero dress and ripped through Paula's hair, while flying beach sand stung her face and arms.

Josh was leaving the shelter of his car to meet her. Behind them, the candle- and lamplit Castle Sturmvögel seemed to rise out of the rocky beach.

'What goes on?' he shouted. 'I thought you must have broken down along the road. We were supposed to eat at Otto's — or had you forgotten? Get in!'

'I'll use my own transport. Follow me, Josh. I'll be OK.'

When he began to argue with her, she all but screamed at him. 'Don't argue, Josh! I'll need my pick-up for work in the morning.'

On the way back to Lüderitz, Paula could barely see the road in front of her, and she felt cold. When they arrived at her cottage, Josh got out of his car, his eyes went over her and he laughed unkindly.

'Well, by the looks of things, I might have saved myself the trouble. You've been having a great time with the count, apparently. We were supposed to have dinner, but obviously your hunger lay in quite another direction. Tell me, was he good? What's he got that I haven't? A Bavarian *schloss*, complete with moat?'

Provoked beyond endurance, Paula lifted her hand and slapped his face.

'Don't you dare talk to me like that, Josh—but in any case, thank you for your concern, by coming to look for me. I might have broken down, as it happens.'

'Thanks for nothing!' He all but spat the words at her as he put his hand to his cheek. Going back to his car, he got in and slammed the door. 'Thanks for nothing!' he shouted again. 'So be it, Paula.'

Later, as she brushed her hair, Paula gazed at herself in the mirror. Dispassionately she noticed that at this moment she was indeed stunningly beautiful. She went on studying her face—the high cheekbones, generous mouth and wide-spaced turquoise-blue eyes, which seemed to be glittering. Her skin glowed and her hair fell about untidily, but looked wonderful. Although she and Karl had not actually made love, she had responded to his lips and searching hands—ready to accept him, and even after the hideous drive from the castle it still showed.

'Is this what you want?' She spoke aloud. 'To end up sleeping with Karl while you're both in Namibia?'

As she got into bed, she began to ask herself if that was really all it would have meant to him.

CHAPTER SIX

IT WAS said by many that Lüderitz should be experienced inwardly and emotionally. Well, thought Paula, that was exactly what was happening to her, especially since meeting Karl von Buren.

Her thoughts were certainly chaotic as she drove along the rough road to the Castle Sturmvögel. Kobus and Johnny were eager to talk about the funeral which had taken place the day before, and she tried to focus on what they were saying as they shared the front seat together.

By the time they reached Agate Beach, she had made up her mind that there was no way she could face Karl and, dropping the men off and explaining that she would call back for them in the afternoon, she went back to her office.

Much to her relief, there was no sign of Karl when she returned for the men in the afternoon.

Still feeling emotionally and physically spent the following morning, she again decided to drop the men off and returned to her office, where she found herself hoping that Karl would turn up to talk things over, but the day went by without a sign of him. Eventually, the whole situation built up to the point where she dreaded to return to work—unless, of course, she broke the contract.

As she drove to the cottages of the handymen the next day, seagulls and cormorants skimmed the misty wavetops and circled over the moored boats in the harbour. On the way out of the little town, which was built on crystalline igneous rock, Paula gazed at the quaint art nouveau and German imperial-style buildings and asked herself how much longer she would be here.

What happened after she had parked the pickup was something like a play, she found herself thinking later. She was one of the cast of characters, Karl was another, and so was the girl with him, a girl with finely chiselled features, smooth blonde hair and almost pale green eyes. Looking at this vision, Paula felt stunned, and to hide her pain she tried to control the muscles of her face so that she could smile. Vaguely she was aware of being introduced by Karl.

The girl's name was Hilda Kirsche and, glamorous in every way, she exuded self-confidence and, like Karl's, her accent was pronounced and attractive.

'Ah, Paula—the girl who owns a cement-mixer!' Hilda laughed lightly. 'It is the first time I have met a girl who has invested in a cement-mixer. Opals, emeralds, diamonds and furs I can understand— but Paula, I do nevertheless admire your courage.' The words carried an undertone of spite.

Hilda was wearing designer jeans and an ivory silk shirt and a lot of clanking silver and jade jewellery.

'Karl and I have been walking on the beach,' she went on, 'in all this fog. I am feeling quite damp! I keep asking myself why Horst von Buren built a castle on this desolate coastline.'

'Well, after all, the great navigator Bartolomeu Dias did call it the sands of hell,' Paula replied stiffly.

Linking both her hands through Karl's arm, Hilda smiled up at him. 'I much prefer the *schloss*, Karl.' She turned to look at Paula. 'Paula, it is something out of a fairy-tale—snow and all!'

Traitor! Paula was thinking a little wildly. You told me you loved me, but obviously you didn't mean it—but then you did say that you hadn't come to Namibia for the impossible to happen—to meet a girl. . . Well, you already *had* a girl, didn't you? Soon, you said, I will have to lie to you!

'I hope,' Hilda was saying, without sincerity, 'you are enthusiastic about your day? What a daunting way to earn a living!'

Karl casually removed Hilda's hands from his arm. 'Hilda turned up yesterday. . .'

'Completely surprising him, of course,' Hilda cut in. 'You see, I wanted to make sure he was behaving himself. Perhaps, Paula, *you* can shed some light on this?' She gave Paula a totally false smile.

'It depends on what you call behaving himself,

Hilda, but I'm sure he's been behaving—as usual.'
Even to her own ears, Paula's voice sounded like
ice. 'Why don't you ask him?'

'Allow me to warn you,' Karl sounded frankly
annoyed, 'ask no questions and you will hear no
lies.'

'You know, it was quite something getting here.'
Hilda's voice was edged with hostility and her
green eyes were hard. 'I caught a regular flight
from Windhoek, where I arrived, to Lüderitz. What
an odd little airfield you have here—and as for
Lüderitz. . .' She laughed. 'It is like the end of the
earth! Anyway, someone I met on the plane gave
me a lift in the car which was there waiting for him
and he drove me all the way to Sturmvögel. He is
a charming man and has something to do with
Consolidated Diamond Mines. He is on a short
visit to Lüderitz.'

'Hilda always succeeds in making a plan,' Karl
looked at Paula, 'and always to her own advantage.
Hein, Hilda?'

'*And* I also have learned to make fairly accurate
judgements, and it is my belief that Paula is a hard
worker.' Hilda's pale green eyes flickered over
Paula. 'Please don't let us keep you.'

Paula glanced at her watch. 'Yes, I can't stand
here talking all morning. These days I find there's
even a deadline when it comes to making trivial
conversation.'

In the days to come, Paula's thoughts festered

and she found herself loathing Karl, especially on those occasions when he sought her out—only to explain that he and Hilda would be going out somewhere.

First it was a yacht trip, lasting about three hours, from where they would be able to admire the views of Lüderitz and its numerous bays. After this trip, Hilda raved to Paula about the penguin colony on Halifax Island, of which they had a view from the yacht. The dolphins, she explained, behaved playfully near the bow of the yacht.

She and Karl also visited the museum, the crayfish factories and the Karakul carpet weavery.

Paula was working alone one morning when Karl came to speak to her. Giving her a level look, he said, 'I never seem to get the chance to talk to you.'

She kept her face expressionless. 'What is it, Karl?' she asked.

'It is only natural that Hilda wishes to sightsee. . .'

'Well, that hardly concerns me,' Paula interrupted. 'In case you're open to a suggestion, though, why don't you take her to see Spitzkoppe? It's known as the Matterhorn of Namibia. It might remind her of your skiing days together on the Alpine slopes—and you, of course.'

'I'm not asking for advice,' he answered angrily. 'I came here to tell you that I want you to take time off to join us in searching for desert roses. After all, you were the one who told me about them.'

Paula looked at him in amazement, then suddenly she laughed. 'I don't know how you define this invitation to yourself, Karl, but I think you have a nerve! I have no intention of joining you and Hilda. As it happens, I've *had* the experience of looking for desert roses.'

'I had planned to do this with you,' he said quietly.

'Well, that was a mistake, wasn't it?' Paula's blue eyes were frankly hostile. 'You'll just have to plan again.'

'Paula, don't be difficult! I also would like you to visit Kolmanskop with us.'

' "Paula, don't be difficult!" You can't be serious?' She flung down the tile-cutter she had been using, since she was working in a room which was being converted into another bathroom. 'Don't come here and waste my time, Karl. You know as well as I do that I have no intention of tagging along with you and Hilda Kirsche. Sightsee with her as much as you like. It has nothing to do with me, except for the fact that I allowed you to make a fool of me.'

She saw his face harden with anger.

'It is time we talked. There are some things we have to straighten out here.'

'There's nothing to straighten out. I allowed you to deceive me. It won't happen again. It's as simple as that.'

When she tried to move away from him, he stepped in front of her. 'Let's not play games, Paula. Hilda took it on her own shoulders to come to Namibia. She is not here at my invitation.'

'That's the last subject I want to talk about, Karl. As for going to search for desert roses, count me out. I'm surprised you had the audacity to ask!'

'I won't take no for an answer. In fact, I have obtained the necessary permit from the DNC offices!' A muscle had tightened in his cheek, and the change in his grey eyes told her that her remark had stung him.

'Well, that's your problem. By the way, did you find the cheque I left on your desk—for the Herero dress?'

'Yes, I did, and I put it where it belonged—in the waste-paper basket.'

'Looking back, Karl, one or two violins would have added a nice touch the other evening. . .even on tape,' she told him. 'Do think about this—and do be careful. It would be terrible if you broke Hilda's back—and your own, of course—by slipping in that old-fashioned bath.'

Thoroughly exasperated, he said, 'I have already explained, I have never done that to any woman before, and I have no desire to repeat the experience.'

'Do I detect that I am intruding?' Hilda's silky voice came as a shock to them both.

Clad in her working clothes and covered in tile

dust, Paula was acutely aware of the other girl's elegant green trouser-suit, which matched her eyes, and her exquisite make-up.

'Yes, Hilda? What is it?' Karl spoke abruptly.

'I was wondering whether we could search for desert roses today, instead of going to look at the lighthouse? Or would that be asking too much, with all that's going on around here?' Hilda's look towards Paula was insinuating.

'Make up your mind for the lighthouse,' snapped Karl, 'because that is where we are going.'

'Very well.' Hilda's voice was frigid. 'If that is what you wish.' Turning to look at Paula again, she said, 'You must have been to look for these roses, surely? However, Karl seemed to think you would nevertheless be coming with us.'

'Karl was wrong,' Paula told her. 'I'm not.'

'Tell me, Paula,' Hilda's voice contained relief, 'are they very deep beneath the surface of the sand?'

'Sometimes they're on top. Anyway, Hilda, if you don't find any, there's a curio shop in Lüderitz which sells desert roses. You can also buy semi-precious stones, by the bag. Karl knows all about this and how well they can be used to their fullest advantage, especially when one can't buy flowers, to add drama to a setting. I guess you can buy most things in life — even the protected desert rose. I'm surprised, Karl, you didn't buy at least one desert rose for your library.'

Karl chose to ignore this sarcasm, but the message in his eyes was explosive.

'I cannot imagine myself digging,' Hilda went on. 'I suppose spades are provided? Don't tell me we have to take our own?'

'Spades would damage concealed roses. You use your hands. You see, although the desert rose looks tough enough, it can easily be damaged,' Paula added for Karl's benefit. 'So you use your hands and — oh, you're allowed two hours, but then a lot can happen in two hours. I hope you enjoy yourself. By the way, Karl, I do hope searching for sand roses comes up to your expectations.'

As she reminded him of his words to her, Karl's eyes reflected the insult.

'If I *do* damage one of these roses,' he answered shortly, 'it will not have been my intention.'

Later in the week, Karl staggered Paula by requesting that she should visit the ghost town of Kolmanskop, and Paula surprised herself even more by accepting the invitation.

'Why not?' Her voice was caustic. 'If nothing else it will be in the interest of reviving my enthusiasm when it comes to my book. You do have the necessary permit from the CDM office, I take it?'

Paula sensed Hilda's resentment immediately she got into the Land Rover. 'I'm surprised you are taking time off from work, Paula,' she said sweetly. She laughed. 'Your cement-mixer will be out of action today!'

'They were taken on a tour of the ghost mining town, Kolmanskop, which was named after Johnny Kolman, a transport driver who had regularly camped near a hillock, and who had to be rescued when his oxen disappeared during a vicious sandstorm.

'Imagine a team of oxen becoming lost in a sandstorm,' Karl remarked, looking at Paula. 'As you have often pointed out, this happened also to men.'

She noticed how his grey eyes went over her designer jeans and attractive T-shirt, which had a Paris label attached to the inside of the neckline.

'It was all a case of fate, I suppose.' She shrugged her shoulders and continued to look unfriendly.

This sad remnant of the diamond diggings was surrounded by desert sand, and yet at one time, Kolmanskop had been a comfortable village. When it became the centre of the diamond-mining industry, prefabricated wooden buildings with corrugated iron roofs were shipped from Germany. Later these buildings were replaced by solid structures, some of them very elaborate.

Glancing at Karl and Hilda from time to time, Paula was aware of their common German interest in the past, and she felt leftout, jealous. . .and let down.

In most of the buildings the sand had nearly reached the ceilings. There was even a casino, and this two-storey recreation building for the staff of the nearby diamond mine was complete with a theatre which had magnificent acoustics.

The central large hall had a stage and the motifs around the walls were hand-painted. There were the usual theatre masks—one smiling and the other with a turned-down mouth.

'Note the turned-down mouth!' Karl's voice was soft and sarcastic as he looked at Paula. 'It rings a bell, no?' His eyes went to her mouth.

She stared back at him with the withering hate of the moment. 'Well, the sad one seems to have won, anyway. After all this grandeur,' she gestured with her hand, 'Kolmanskop had to be left to the mercy of the desert.'

As she spoke she was again aware of his eyes going over her understated outfit. She had taken incredible pains when dressing and knew she looked glamorous.

'This is the ultimate tragedy,' he went on, looking around. 'All the buildings share the same fate—that of being placed in a relentless desert, where nothing is allowed to survive. It is obvious that the winds carry flying sand which piles up and wears away everything.' He turned to look at her. 'Something like distrust—and even jealousy, perhaps?'

Paula's beautiful face was angry as she stared back at him.

'Like jealousy, yes, and distrust. Something always causes it. In this case, those winds and flying sand have succeeded in blowing gaping holes right through everything.'

Hilda had left them, reluctantly, to go and talk to a young couple who had beckoned to her.

'Paula,' Karl's eyes contained anger, 'I hope you are enjoying this, because I am not! Don't let's have this double-talk. It is senseless.'

'Yes, it *is* senseless. It's as senseless as the wars you mentioned which somehow were triggered off. *This* is a war. *You* created it! Now, let's talk about Kolmanskop!' Her voice was brittle. 'Talking about wars — wars are crazy, and World War One was no exception. It resulted in *this* — what you see here, now. A slump in diamond sales shortly afterwards, followed by the lingering death of Kolmanskop until not one person remained — only these buildings which were fated to be ravaged by sand and more and more sand and scorching desert winds. I suppose, in between all this, though, the people would have had a roaring time. They would have gone wild in this very same casino and they would have gone home afterwards to make useless love — including my fickle great-grandfather. I don't suppose, like Johnny Kolman's oxen, he got lost in a desert sandstorm at all. He possibly cleared off somewhere with this dame.'

'Maybe you are being too hard on him — but then you have led me to believe, in no uncertain terms, that you consider most men to be rats.'

'Believe it or not, I didn't always think this way.

That was probably my big mistake in life.' She gave
Karl a hostile look. 'How nice for you to turn up in
Namibia to find me here—just laid on for your
amusement while you were wedged here between
the Atlantic and the bleak desert. I was to play a
useful role in your selfish life while you were cut
off from the jet-set, wasn't I?'

'Did you agree to come here today just to carry
on with this war? Let me tell you something,
Paula,' his steel-grey eyes began to take her apart,
'being wedged between the Atlantic and the bleak
desert does not particularly worry me, coming as I
do from Bavaria, where the *schloss* is virtually
imprisoned between mountains and forests. In the
winters we are practically buried in snow. The
moat turns to ice, the sun is hidden from us from
behind the mountains. We become, in fact, totally
isolated, so don't talk to me about being wedged
between the Atlantic and the desert and panting
for some woman to make life bearable for me!'

'Oh, go away!' Paula's face was full of hate now.
'I don't like you!'

When Karl approached her several days later about
taking a trip into the desert, she looked at him in
astonishment.

'Are you seriously asking me to tag along with
you and Hilda *again*? What do you take me for—a
rhinoceros, some thick-skinned animal?'

'Permit me, Paula, to remind you that we had

discussed this. The main thing here is that there will now be three of us. In other words, you will not be alone with me, should you come. You will be able to carry on with your research in complete safety!' His eyes were hard.

'I don't want to go, Karl! Whether there are three or six people, I don't want to go!'

Completely ignoring her remark, he went on, 'I suggest you explain to your handymen that they take a few days off. I am sure they will have no objection to this bonus.'

'*You* suggest!' Paula took a long impatient breath and shook her head. 'Allow me to point out, Karl, that any bonus in the way of a few days off work will come from me!'

'That is entirely up to you—but I am closing Sturmvögel for the period I have in mind.'

Paula looked at him lividly. 'Why are you including me in something which concerns you and Hilda? It's Hilda who wants to sightsee. The fact that you mentioned this trip to me before she arrived means nothing. If you want to close your castle, that's fine with me. Close it. It's not a problem. I have work to do for Josh, anyway. I'm surprised, though, that you intend closing Sturmvögel, since you've always led me to believe that these repairs are to be treated as urgent. I'm also surprised that you didn't think to entrust Herr Heinrich with the keys. I'm sure he could have taken time off to spend a few days here to keep an eye on me and my ex-fishermen while you're away.'

'Since you thought fit to drag Heinrich's name up, let me say that it was his suggestion that we stay at a farmhouse right on the edge of the desert. These people are friends of his, and he has already spoken to them about us.'

'Really? A farm, no less? What do they grow there, on the edge of the desert? Asparagus? Succulent green peas? Luscious peaches — or flowers, for the international market, maybe?'

He turned away from her for a moment, and sighed with impatience. Swinging round again, he said, 'Why don't you *think* before you go on like this? *Hein*? Sometimes I feel like shaking you! It is a stud farm, but you do not give me time to finish. It will take us the best part of a day to reach this stud farm which is near to part of a nature conservation area. The owners, Heinrich tells me, bought a dilapidated turn-of-the-century house on land which, many years ago, used to be a stud farm. Now it is once again being built up and is fast becoming successful. These people have a four-seater plane which they fly here to pick up Heinrich, and when the guest-house has been completed and officially opened the plane will serve to transport guests. This entire trip and set-up could be interesting for you. Surely I do not have to point this out to you?'

Since she had slicked her hair right back, Paula's

blue eyes looked huge in her pale face. She was feeling exhausted and could feel her own paleness. In fact, only this morning she had thought how weary she looked. . .how sad and full of misery. This intensified her anger towards Karl.

'Ah, a stud farm. Horses, then, on the edge of the desert?

'What is it with you?' Karl shouted in exaspera-tion. 'There are times when your nature is far too intricate for me to try even to understand!'

'Well, don't try.' She hated herself for being so childish.

'Yes, horses on the edge of the desert, and it is not the first time. What about, for instance, the wild horses of Namibia? Where do you think these horses originated from? Speculation has it that they once belonged to surrounding farms, from where they ran wild into the desert—and so, my dear Paula, there have been, and still are, horses, before today.'

'Speculation also has it, Karl, that the horses you speak of—the wild horses—are descendants of the cavalry mounts left behind by the German Schutztruppe during the First World War.'

'I am quite aware of that theory,' he pointed out. 'I don't need you to enlighten me. Once again, how any of these horses have been able to survive such harsh and hostile conditions, often waterless, is a riddle I am not in a position to solve—but there they are, and there also happens to be the stud farm to which I have referred. Hilda or no Hilda, I want you to come. I know you want to come, so why do you persist in beating about the bush? Speaking about Hilda, I did not ask her to come out here. She came of her own accord. I have already told you that. Apart from how I feel about this, I have decided to play host and have agreed to show her places of interest before she goes back home.'

After a long moment Paula asked, 'How will we go there?'

'Complete with maps and food for the road, we will go in my Land Rover. We will leave here in the early morning and arrive there towards sunset.'

Paula took an unsettled breath. 'How does— Hilda feel about this?'

'Who knows what Hilda feels?' Karl shrugged.

'I'll think about it.' Paula's expression was closed.

'I want your answer now! I have to make plans.'

Why not use him, Paula thought, as he had tried to use her? As he had pointed out, it would be interesting.

'I'll come,' she said, shoving to one side the dismal thought that Karl and Hilda would probably be sharing a room at the stud farm.

'Good.' His eyes held hers. 'I'll speak to you later about the arrangements.'

After he had gone, Paula massaged her aching temples. Quite suddenly she felt she had to be out in the open, and she decided to take a break on the beach. Maybe she would even go home later.

She was engrossed in examining some of the plant life which clung to the sand when Hilda's voice startled her.

'So you are taking a break from your labours, Paula?' She got down beside Paula. 'These flowers are like little yellow puffs, don't you think?'

Trying not to show her frustration, Paula said, 'Yes, they are.'

'I am given to understand by Karl that we will be driving into that terrible desert. I wanted to sight-see, but I'm not so sure about this.' Hilda glanced at Paula. 'I understand, also, that you will be going.'

'I said I'd go, yes. I'll be making notes for a book I intend writing. Besides, we won't see anything like it after we get back home. It should be quite an experience. I haven't managed to get around much since I've been here.'

'And so, Paula, you have not been anywhere — with Karl?'

'No.'

There was a cold silence, then Hilda went on, 'Karl must, of course, be familiar with your cottage?'

'No, he isn't, actually.' Paula's voice was cool.

'Really? In the circumstances, I find that strange.' Beside Paula, Hilda trailed the fragrance of some exotic perfume.

'It's a very private cottage, Hilda,' Paula told her. 'I'm a very private person.'

'But seeing that he. . .'

As he came on the scene, Karl's voice broke into Hilda's sentence. 'This looks like a mothers' meeting,' he commented.

'We were talking about going into the desert.' Hilda plucked one of the yellow puffs and stroked her cheek with it.

Paula stood up and dusted the sand from her jeans. 'I was just about to break the meeting up.' She had loosened her flaming auburn hair, and it fell to her shoulders and blew about in the wind.

As she also stood up Hilda said, 'I have been thinking, we will have to watch our complexions in the desert, especially, I should imagine, you, Paula. The kind of work you are doing must surely be taking its toll, as it is. I have had my own skin analysed for specific problems and have, thank goodness, been assured that my skin is flawless.' She laughed lightly. 'Woman to woman, I suggest you indulge in a facial, at least, from time to time.'

Paula felt her temper rising. 'The French, I believe, call having a facial a luxurious necessity.' She managed to keep her voice honey-sweet. 'At the moment there's no time for these luxurious necessities, but it won't be long now before I pack up here and go home, where I'll pamper myself.'

'So you intend to go home shortly?' Hilda's eyes narrowed.

'Yes. By the way, Hilda, I've also been thinking...you'd look great in a Herero dress, especially with your flawless skin. You should get Karl to buy you one.'

'They are not to my taste, thank you. I have seen them in Windhoek. And you, Paula, do you have one?'

'At the back of my wardrobe somewhere.' Paula glanced at her watch. 'Oh, by the way, Karl, I should have mentioned—I'm going off now. I'll call back for the ex-fishermen, later this afternoon.'

'Are you not feeling well?' He sounded genuinely concerned. 'This morning, earlier, you looked very pale.'

'I'm fine. I have a date, actually,' she explained.

'That sounds romantic.' Hilda sounded almost friendly. 'Where are you going—or am I being rude?'

'We're having lunch—at the water's edge,' Paula lied, hating herself for the way in which she was carrying on.

'Who is he, Paula?'

'He's an artist, Hilda.'

'Well, don't let us keep you.' Karl's grey eyes were hard. 'Enjoy your lunch—at the water's edge.'

'Thank you, I will.'

CHAPTER SEVEN

THREE days later, by the time Karl had parked the Land Rover, Paula had locked the door to her cottage and was on her way down the path. The air smelled of kelp, and she tilted her face to the cool caress of the mist and found it hard to believe that within a short distance lay what could only be described as a hot thirstland—a place of changing landscapes, desolate rock, gravel desert, shifting sands and dunes.

After the arrangements for the excursion to the stud farm had been finalised, Paula had decided to update her book-keeping at the office and had not had occasion to see Karl. The break from his company was what she needed, she told herself.

Karl was already out of the Land Rover, and he reached for her bag. His eyes went over her honey-coloured fisherman's jersey, made from the finest cashmere, to her well-cut designer jeans.

'Good morning, Paula.' His manner was brusque.

'Hi.' Paula's eyes went to the front seat. 'Where's Hilda?'

'Hilda is not coming.'

She gave him a blank look. 'What do you mean,

Hilda's not coming? She was supposed to be coming to this stud farm, wasn't she? Don't tell me you've left her in that castle alone, Karl?'

'Why is it, Paula, that you always jump to so many conclusions?' he snapped. 'Hilda had a visit from the man she met on the plane coming to Lüderitz who, to use her own words, has something to do with Consolidated Diamond Mines. The outcome of this visit was that Hilda decided to leave with him for Windhoek, and she is therefore on her first stage back home.'

'But what happened? There must have been a good reason!'

'The reason was, we had a long-overdue bust-up. Is that not what they say?'

Paula's expression began to tighten. 'Had this anything to do with me? That is, with the fact that I was tagging along on this trip? Why didn't you let me know?'

'Get in. What does it matter?' Karl exploded angrily. 'What did you think I would do? Try to stop her from leaving? She came here of her own free will and she left the same way. Look, I don't intend discussing this on the pavement.'

Paula tried to hold on to her temper. 'No, I will *not* get in! This changes everything. In other words, I'm not going . Give me back my bag.'

He made an impatient gesture. 'What are you afraid of? You showed enough interest before Hilda arrived. What, then, is the problem?'

'The problem is that a lot of unpleasant water has flowed under the bridge since I last showed interest in this trip.'

'Why are we wasting time here?' Opening the door of the Land Rover, Karl all but threw her case into the back. 'Let's get going, if we are to reach this stud farm before nightfall — but, just for the record, Hilda and I were washed up a long time ago, only she wouldn't recognise the fact. Come along, get in, Paula.'

'This changes everything,' she insisted. 'You seem to forget, Karl, that you've given me ample reason to believe that I can't trust you. For that matter, Hilda didn't appear to trust you either. She said she'd come to Namibia to make sure you were behaving yourself. She must have had two reasons for saying that — one, that you were not washed up, as you say, and two, that she couldn't trust you out of her sight.'

'My interest in Hilda, believe it or not, was over a considerable time ago. We met on a skiing holiday in the Alps, and our relationship lasted no longer than those two weeks. To get back to the fact that there will now be just the two of us, I will not make you do anything you do not want to do. I told you that, from the beginning, before Hilda arrived. That still stands — unpleasant water having run under the bridge or not.'

While he was speaking, Paula found herself thinking that they had been about to make love before Josh had turned up that night. Yet here she was, throwing all caution to the winds just by standing here arguing with Karl, which meant that she was considering going.

'We are not going to let these friends of Heinrich's down,' said Karl. 'They are expecting us. Get in, Paula—and for once, shut up!'

All of a sudden, no decisions were required of her, for *he* had made them, simply by having thrown her case into the Land Rover, so she got in.

As he got in beside her and started the engine he said, 'Hilda and I met at a ski-resort. . .but you had already gathered that, of course.'

'Yes, I had, since that's your lifestyle.' Paula's voice was riddled with sarcasm.

'I was infatuated,' he went on. 'We. . .'

'In other words,' she cut in, 'you were foolishly enamoured, is that it? Is that all it amounted to? Is that the only reason that girl came out here?'

He turned angrily. 'Yes, in other words, I was foolishly enamoured. Put it whatever way you wish. She was also infatuated, but this infatuation had more to do with my family history than anything else. There is a hard shell about Hilda, and at the back of everything with her, there was the title, the *schloss*—very conveniently and romantically raised in pink stone and part of it going back to the fifteenth century. There was the coat of arms, the ancestral hall, the banqueting hall, the family heirlooms—and even the moat!'

'And how convenient for you that she's not here to defend herself!' Paula's voice carried contempt now. 'I think we'd better change the subject.'

'So you think we must not talk about Hilda — when Hilda concerns us? Your great-grandfather is not here to defend himself, and yet you have done nothing else but express the opinion that he was just a typical male and had possibly cleared off with some woman. Anyway, let's not have any fights about Hilda before we even start on the journey.'

Once they had left the sand-scoured streets of Lüderitz behind, they continued in silence, while Paula gazed at the changing landscape. The fog was beginning to lift as the sun penetrated it. She began to discard her honey-coloured jersey. Beneath it she was wearing a cotton top of the same shade.

Karl turned to watch her. 'Do you want me to stop the Land Rover?'

'No. I can manage, thank you.'

Sand lay across the tarmac road and there was now harsh desert on either side. In places the sand was either spectacular red or white, and the heat was shimmering. After a while, there were road signs warning against the danger of the legendary horses which had adapted themselves to harsh desert conditions.

'Why aren't you taking notes?' asked Karl.

'I'm relying on my photographic memory, but I

intend making notes. After all, that's the only reason I happen to be here,' Paula added.

He turned to look at her. 'The only reason?' She heard the mockery behind the words.

'Yes, Karl, the only reason.'

'And you just want to make sure I know the score, is that it? Look, Paula, I am aware of the points in this game.'

A moment or two later, he slackened speed. 'It looks as if we are in luck. They must be the legendary wild horses of Namibia Sperrgebiet — perhaps the only wild horses in the world, in fact.' He stopped the Land Rover. 'Heinrich was telling me that these horses drink sometimes only once in five or six days. Apparently there is only one water supply which they must visit when they are not grazing. This water is pumped from a borehole for their benefit.'

He drove on slowly and then stopped again and, without thinking, Paula moved closer to him so that she could see the horses on his side better. Her face was close to his and she could smell the lotion he'd used after shaving.

Soon afterwards they hit a terrible stretch of corrugations and there were rocks lying all over the place. At one stage, a great gust of wind suddenly hit the Land Rover.

The desert, thought Paula, at first impressed, then fascinated and finally awed, until travelling,

especially for the driver, became a trial of endurance. The sky seemed vast.

When they approached a lonely, derelict house
Karl slackened speed again and then stopped to
refer to his map. Watching him, Paula laughed
outright.

'Don't tell me you're expecting to find *this* on the
map?'

He turned to smile at her. 'I was checking to see
whether we are still in a restricted area, but it's not.
I think this house deserves to have its photograph
taken, don't you? It must surely have a story to
tell, but unfortunately it cannot talk. Shall we get
out and stretch our legs? Let's take a look round.'

As they got out of the Land Rover, they experienced the full blast of the desert heat. It was a kind
of nailing heat, Paula thought, and seemed to be
pinning them down.

Engulfed and ravaged by shifting sand, the small
and distressingly ugly house seemed to be cringing
from that heat. Above the warped and blistered
half-open door there appeared the date — 1913.

Karl had to push and shove the door to open it
further, and it grated along the sand-blasted and
cracked cement floor. Everywhere there was sad
evidence of wind and sand, and it was difficult to
believe that at one time people had lived and, what
was more, loved here, Paula thought.

These thoughts became inconsistent and without
reason or logic. Had Rory Paul Stewart fallen in

love with the daughter—or even the wife, of the man who had owned this house? Was *this* the reason he had become conveniently lost? Once again, looking at Karl, she felt threatened by his good looks and, when it suited him, his charm.

Suddenly she felt a wave of intense, illogical hostility towards him.

'Why on earth would anybody build a house in a hopeless, dismal place like this?' she said. 'Although perhaps it used to be a railway house, but the railway lines have been completely hidden by years and years of blowing sand.'

'Perhaps, on the other hand, this particular area had been fertile—like an oasis—before the desert once again took over something else. I think that, now we have stopped, we will have lunch here a little later. We'll sit in the Land Rover. By the way, be on the alert in here, Paula,' added Karl. 'There might be an adder lurking somewhere.'

'Could there be snakes here?'

'There is always a chance. There's a side-winding adder which travels with high speed over sand dunes. You get sand-dwelling snakes throughout the world, in fact. Their scales resemble the desert sand. They wait in ambush for their prey, just under the surface of the sand, with only the eyes protruding—like the eyes of a crocodile in a river.'

'When it comes to the desert, you're very clued up, aren't you?' Paula remarked.

After a moment he asked quietly, 'Is anything the matter?'

'Why should anything be the matter?'

Abruptly the relaxed feeling which had begun to exist between them seemed to shift.

'I was merely expressing a thought,' Paula went on. 'If you're familiar with the snow-clad slopes of Europe, there's no reason, I suppose, why you shouldn't be familiar with the deserts of the world. You've — judging by the way you talk — probably been to the Sahara and places like Tunisia, Algeria. . .India. You know, I've heart that some people ski on Italian volcanoes.' Her voice was light and bantering, but for some reason or other she was trembling.

There was, she noticed, a cool gleam in Karl's grey eyes. 'To satisfy your curiosity, I *have* been to some of the places you mention. What's the problem, Paula? Why have the old snow-clad Alpine slopes reared their heads again?'

'It's an interesting subject, after all. I'm told that skiing on the dunes is something tourists can now look forward to in Namibia. In its way, that could also prove to be very romantic — another unique experience to be enjoyed by dashing princes and counts, of course.'

'What could be more unique than looking over a derelict desert house with a bad-tempered redhead? Do you wish to take photographs?'

'No. I've left my camera in the Land Rover.

Besides, I'll leave the photos to you. You can always let me have the negatives. You know,' she added, her voice soft, 'a little German family probably lived in this house. Maybe there were diamonds nearby, which seems to have been the downfall of many, including, perhaps, my dear great-grandfather, but in the end what all they ended up with was that scorched, harsh landscape you see out there. Finally they ended up without even that!'

'As I have already pointed out, this might have been a fertile spot — only to be finished off by the encroaching sands and the lack of rain and water,' Karl answered.

'An oasis in the desert wouldn't dry up!' Her voice sounded aggressive to her own ears.

'How do you know?' Karl's tone was irritable.

'Anyway,' she continued, 'in this house the people would have known scorching days and cold nights — whether the area had been fertile or not. I wonder how the sky looks at sunset — or sunrise, for that matter?'

He came over to stand next to her. 'Shall we stop over and find out? Here, there would be no interruptions.' He was watching her as if he found her hightly irritating.

Since they had arrived at this baking hot little house, Karl had suddenly become her enemy again, and she derived satisfaction from baiting him.

'What would they have called this house?' she asked. 'At the moment it's such a miserable place. What would one call it now — Hot Sands?'

'I prefer Desert Rose.' She felt the power of his angry eyes.

'Desert Rose? Perhaps you need to see an optician? There's not a desert rose in sight.' She moved away from him with a kind of feline grace.

'Since I always think of you as a desert rose, I'll keep to that.'

She turned to look at him. 'Really? Why, Karl? Let me guess. . .when you come to think of it, a desert rose is actually quite nondescript.'

'In a certain light they glitter. Sand roses in the Namib are beautiful rosettes of crystal, as you said.'

'Anyway, let's not make a big deal of this,' said Paula. 'One thing I *do* know, though, a desert rose is very brittle and easily damaged.'

'Are you trying to make me feel guilty again? You don't appear to believe me when I tell you that I am in love with you.'

'Let's put it this way — you'd have to give me about ten years to adjust to the possibility that you really mean it!'

Except for an eerie whispering desert breeze, the house was quiet around them.

'You know, Karl,' said Paula, 'I'll often think of this day here with you, after I've left Namibia, that is.'

'When you return to your father and countless

handsome and intelligent admirers?' His voice was hard.

'I might go back to Ireland to see my father, but only for a while. You see, I'm thinking of renting a flat in London and working there. Believe me, I'll choose a place where I can look out on banks of yellow daffodils and terraced roses. I'll have rose bowls all over the place.'

'And the desert rose will be a thing of the past?' He sounded bored and angry at the same time.

'I didn't say that. I'll take mine back with me—and what's more, I may even take a pile of semi-precious stones, which I can use on certain occasions, to create drama. You see, you gave me the idea.' She took a breath and looked around the room. 'Now, let's have lunch. I hope you thought to bring champagne?'

'As you should know by now, I think of everything.' Karl's voice was cold.

While he watched Paula moodily, she made a big show of surveying the room.

'This would make a wonderful country cottage for you. As I see it, Karl, you should have a couple of nice plump sofas here, using a bold floral chintz. . .maybe colours like poppy, Venetian red, orange—or are those colours too hot for you? Rose, maybe, would be nice, or watermelon. One sofa to go over there and the other directly opposite. Since there's no green in sight, how about hunting green, jade green, mint, apple. . . The choice is endless.

Green—for ecology and the green revolution, that sort of thing.'

As if to humour her he said, 'Having two sofas leaves no room for chairs.' He was obviously irritated, though.

'That shouldn't be a problem. I can't see you having many visitors out here—not until you built a guest-house, anyway. But that could be a good thing. You might find you enjoy a sense of solitude. You'll have all the time in the world to carefully plan a bath and supper party. What about a nice brass tray which stands on a black filigree base—like the furniture they use in Indian temples? Brass shouldn't tarnish here. That would just leave room for a small drinks table beneath the window. You could always bring a few cut-glass bottles and crystal glasses along from Sturmvögel.'
She had noticed at once how his grey eyes had reflected the insult at her reference to a bath and supper party.

'Oh, I see it all,' she went on. 'The copper tray on a filigree stand, perhaps even a leather ottoman or two, a brass samovar and the sand lapping at the front door.'

'I noticed a pump outside. Only God knows where it used to pump water from. It probably doesn't work, and so, my dear Paula, I might yet have to drink and bath in mineral water!'

'Another unique experience in store for you.' She turned away, dismayed at what she had started. 'What about something madly different? Jute, tobacco-coloured curtains, for instance? And a jewel-like Persian rug to go between the sofas. . . or would you prefer a sleigh bed? It's your choice, after all.'

After a moment he said, 'Tell me, Paula, how did we get on this kick? Why don't you just call it a day, huh?'

'Not until I've finished. I always make a point of finishing a job, no matter whether I've lost interest or not. I think I've proved that at Sturmvögel, don't you? Look, there's even a fireplace.' She could not seem to stop herself. 'The von Buren coat of arms must certainly go above it—not to mention a tapestry. Leave everything to me, Karl. I'm pretty good when it comes to cement work. I'll get my cement-mixer out here, even if I have to carry it myself. Maybe, on the other hand, I'll really pamper myself and hire a team of oxen. Now, in place of flowers, you simply must bring your private collection of gemstones along and—oh, I'm glad I thought of this—maybe a Herero dress or two. You never know, you might be looking out of the window one day, and see a caravan of camels descending on you, complete with an attractive girl. You know how lucky you are!'

'I am going to the Land Rover to pour myself a glass of mineral water. Do you want some?' She could detect the fury in him.

'Oh, please. My tongue is quite dry.'

'I am sure it is — *and* with reason!' Karl retorted.

By the time he returned, he seemed to have calmed down and spoke in a light casual manner, but she could see that he was still angry.

'That is a world by itself, outside.' He handed her a glass. 'The champagne will keep until we have lunch.'

There was drama in Paula's walk as, after a moment, she took the glass from him and wandered towards the small passage.

'Come and have a look, Karl,' she called out. 'There's a super bathroom.'

When he came to stand behind her she went on in that same brittle voice, 'We'll leave the ball-and-claw bath, I think. It's quite a feature. And by the way, an exotic cactus is a must. I'll arrange for one to come on the ox-wagon. The bath will take a lot of restoring, as you can see, but I'll cope with the enamelling and the tiling. I think — ink-blue here, with a wine-red bath, but then you're the expert when it comes to *baths*.' Beneath her flippantly sarcastic remark, she was devastated that she had brought up the subject.

'Ja. . .Well——' she heard him take a long breath '—once again, since this is what we're getting at here, *that* was a brutal thing to have done that night. Tell me, Paula, are you enjoying yourself? *Hein*?' The last word was soft and almost drawn out as a caress.

With her fingers clamped tightly round her glass,

she turned and gave him a level look. 'Yes. Aren't you?' She knew she was behaving childishly, but she seemed to be possessed by the devil.

'You will get a shock if I decide to beat you at your own game,' he said.

After a stricken moment she said, 'What am I doing here with you, Karl? That's what I keep asking myself. Still, worse things have happened to me, I suppose.'

She left him to go through to the main bedroom. 'This is obviously the main bedroom, and how fortunate it is that it is a step away from the bathroom—just across the narrow passage. Tell me what you think here, Karl. What about sunset colours? You know, fuchsia-pink and gold, for instance?' Against her better judgement she went on, 'A big brass bed would just about fill the room, but it would be well worth it, I think. Much nicer than a heavy four-poster. The possibilities of turning this little room into something quite dramatic are endless. Another thing, do think about having a medallion above the bed, depicting your ancestors.'

'And don't forget the swags of velvet.' Karl's voice was angry now. 'Tied back with thick silk ropes. There must be a large *shrank*, of course. So far as *I* am concerned, *that* is a must!'

She turned to look at him. 'A *shrank*? What's a *shrank*?'

'A *shrank* is a wardrobe in which I will lock you

from time to time, when I can no longer stand your lashing Irish tongue!'

Paula's turquoise eyes watched him as he put his glass on the window-sill and then took hers away from her and placed it next to it.

Grasping her roughly by the shoulders, he said, 'Paula, don't do this! I don't find it amusing or entertaining. You have been out to goad me. You speak so glibly about the *bath*. . .the big brass *bed*. It is a pity these things do not exist, no? Is that what is bothering you? The fact that there is no bed here? The fact that your artist drop-out turned up that particular night in question — is that it?' He was almost shouting now.

When he pulled her towards him and crushed his mouth on hers, all her senses told her, immediately, that she wanted him. The imaginary brass bed became very real — so real, in fact, that it could have been there in the small room and she almost expected him to pick her up and put her there.

'Do you want me to take you here, Paula? Here and now, in this godforsaken little house with its cracked cement floors?' His voice was harsh — so harsh that she pushed him away, with all the strength she possessed.

'You were going to share a bed with Hilda at the stud farm, weren't you? Now that that's fallen flat, you get to work on me!'

Holding her eyes with his own, Karl laughed sarcastically. 'I get to work on you? How exactly did you reach this conclusion? I told you, Hilda went sour on me a long time ago. I had no intention of sharing a bed with her at the stud farm. Certainly we did not share one at Sturmvögel. Why else do you think she left? It was *over*, I tell you!'

'Well, it certainly didn't look as if it was over,' she retorted. 'All those little excursions together — the yachting trip, from where you could both admire views of Lüderitz and the bays, the penguin colony on Halifax Island, the museum, the crayfish factories, the Karakul weavery. . .'

'While you remained behind at Sturmvögel, is that it?'

'You forgot to add — dressed like a stevedore!'

'Why is it that you keep reminding me what I said? What I did? Look, Paula, you attract me more than any other girl I have every known. I wanted you that night, and I want you now — just as you want me.'

He reached for her again and his hands moved down the length of her back, drawing her closer to him until he jean-clad legs were crushed against the warmth of his. She felt the surge of primitive pleasure that he had aroused in her before.

His hands went up beneath the cotton top she was wearing, so that he could move them intimately over the small lacy bra she was wearing, and she felt a sense of helpless drifting and turned her face to his, searching hungrily for his mouth.

'I don't know where this is going to end.' Karl's

voice was hoarse. 'The floor? On the hot sands outside — or just standing here? I think not, my darling!'

Vaguely, at the back of things, Paula was aware of the intense heat and the wind which had got up and seemed to be shaking the small house to its very foundations. It was growing dark. . .

When a window began to slam backwards and forwards in the house somewhere, Karl drew back quickly.

'What the devil is going on? It's one hell of a sandstorm, Paula!' he shouted. 'And I've left the doors of the Land Rover open. I'll be back in a minute.'

Paula looked out of the window. There was a full-scale sandstorm outside. The sun had become a point of hazy light and it was obliterated as the wind gathered more and more sand from the desert. She had visions of Karl becoming lost — like Johnny Kolman's oxen on the hillock outside Kolmanskop.

'Karl!' she shouted, as she ran down the passage and thinking of her great-grandfather this time, who had disappeared without a trace. 'Karl darling, where are you?'

He had just come back into the house. 'Would you believe that? I almost choked to death out there. I could hardly breathe!'

'I was frantic!' she told him. 'I thought you'd just disappeared. How's the Land Rover?'

He laughed. 'Looking a bit like Kolmanskop, but fine, otherwise. I've closed the windows—a bit late, but still. . .'

He took her into his arms and looked into her eyes.

'What we had going a few moments ago had no future, after all.' He kissed her and then drew back. 'It is urgent, this matter, but it can wait, no?' He put his hands on either side of her face and kissed her again.

The sandstorm was passing. The light on one side of the landscape was almost black, while the other was sunny and bright. The Land Rover now stood in the light.

'We'll have lunch,' Karl was saying, 'enjoy our champagne and then be on our way.'

CHAPTER EIGHT

EUPHORBIA succulents stood on either side of the gates to the Stud Farm Mirabilis.

Karl got out of the Land Rover to open and then close the gates. Getting back into the vehicle, he gave Paula a searching look. 'Well, I guess this is it. Are you tired?'

'No, not really, but it was a relief when the terrain started changing. Although it's still very dry, it's become interesting, don't you think?' There was a hint of tension in her voice.

Karl sat back and moved his shoulders. 'Heinrich mentioned those succulents at the gates. Apparently the milk sap is used by the indigenous people for medicinal and magical purposes, not to mention as an arrow poison. All this I find difficult to understand.' Changing his position, he leaned over to kiss her. 'All I know is—it's magic to be here with you.'

After a moment she said, 'And you know, that's precisely what worries me. It *is* magic, Karl. I shouldn't have come—I'm beginning to realise that.'

'What are you talking about now?' His voice was suddenly cold.

Before she answered, Paula sighed. 'Karl, there's a vast difference between being in love, mere sexual passion, and magical spells.'

'It is interesting to speculate why it is you still don't trust me. Anyway, as I see it, sexual passion plays its part in love.'

She waited for his anger to cool before she answered. 'I fully realise that it might not have seemed like it in that derelict house, but I'm a very careful person. Now that we're here, I've come to my senses. I must be frank with you—I have no intention of permitting a magic spell to get to work on me while we're here. In other words, I'm not going to delude myself that these few days happen to be some kind of counterfeit holiday for newlyweds.'

His steel-grey eyes were hard. 'I have asked you to marry me.'

'I know, but—well, I haven't all that much to go on, except that I'm fully aware that you lead an exciting life.'

'Particularly when it comes to the Alpine slopes, is that it?' As he put the Land Rover into motion he went on, 'It is always a mistake, Paula, to try to rake up someone's past, especially when you have no knowledge of that past. Except for what I have told you, you know nothng about me.'

'And don't you see? That's what worries me. Your past *does* concern me. I have a right to ask myself a lot of questions.'

For a few moments he seemed to be giving his full attention to the poor condition of the road which would take them to the home of Ella and Max Richter.

'Now that we've arrived here, you have become apprehensive — especially after what happened at that desert-choked house today. Don't choke things for us, Paula, with doubts about my feelings for you.' His voice was quiet and coldly angry. 'Some time before Hilda arrived and we were discussing the possibility of doing something like this, I mentioned that I would not expect anything of you which you did not want to give. That still stands. What do you take me for? I have no intention of forcing myself on you.'

Paula turned to look at him. 'Well, that's all right, then.' The tone of her voice matched his. 'Please try to see my side of this, though. I don't want to jump into something I'll be sorry for later.'

During the last stretch of their one-day journey, the terrain had changed, and so had the light. In the approaching glow of sunset, everything looked very dramatic. The land was surrounded by distant and barren hills, which seemed to have been created from piled-up shapes resembling ancient Egyptian pyramids. Large weatherbeaten stones appeared to be actually growing out of the light-coloured and arid soil. Stunted thorn trees grew right next to the boulders and often right through them, while small stones were strewn everywhere.

In places, however, the earth was covered by stunted scrub.

Paula's troubled eyes seemed drawn to a small fenced-in cemetery, and a shudder passed through her. People, she thought, lived out here, and if they died out here they were buried out here. . .or at least, before the days of privately owned light aircraft.

Max and Ella Richter had obviously been looking out for the Land Rover, and soon after Karl had parked it they were on the scene.

Introductions were casual and friendly, then Ella asked, 'But where is your fiancée, Karl? I hope nothing has happened to—Hilda? Heinrich mentioned her name, of course.'

Paula immediately felt herself tensing at Ella's description of Hilda. Herr Heinrich must have referred to Hilda as Karl's fiancée—and why? Because he had known this to be the case.

'At the last moment Hilda decided to leave for Windhoek.' Karl did not seem to feel it necessary to correct Ella, Paula noticed. 'From there she will begin her journey back home. There was nothing wrong. She just wanted to go back.'

'A room has been prepared for the two young ladies.' Ella glanced at Paula. 'It is a large room, and I hope, Paula, you will be comfortable and not feel too lost in it, without Hilda to keep you company?'

'I'm sure I'll be very comfortable,' Paula answered politely. 'Thank you, Ella.'

They were shown by Max and Ella to their rooms in the original old house, which had been built in 1908 and was still in the process of being restored to act as a separate guest-house. Its turn-of-the-century German architectural style was strangely out of context with the arid harshness of the surrounding bare hills and parched conditions.

The room which had been prepared for two was indeed large and the space interrupted by three wide arches. These arches framed three huge windows. In the dying light, the ground-level view alone was almost romantic. A private bathroom led off the bedroom.

'This was one of the first farmhouses to have electricity,' Ella explained to Paula. 'Within a few years it had—and still has, of course—its own generator.' Laughing lightly, she added, 'It was also one of the first houses to have flush toilets. When you have freshened up come to the main house where, to welcome you to Stud Farm Mirabilis, drinks will be served. Karl is just across the corridor from you. You will both bear with us, I'm sure, when you notice the many closed doors and signs of workmen all around you. The guest-house has not been officially opened and so far Heinrich has been our only guest. We have arranged for work to stop, though, during the few days you will be here. By the way, Paula, I wish you luck with your book. This visit should fill in all the gaps, according to Heinrich.'

Paula's thoughts were active, on what Ella had had to say with regard to the book she intended writing, as she had a wash and applied fresh make-up, then changed quickly into a pair of black trousers and a turquoise top. A bath would have to wait until bedtime, she thought as she combed her auburn hair back from her face and arranged it into a chignon. As she and Karl had arrived later than was expected, it seemed unfair to keep the Richters waiting.

When she opened her door she found Karl doing the same thing, just across the corridor.

'Great minds think alike,' he mocked. 'How are you back there? Are you happy with your room?'

'Yes. Would you like to take a look before we go? It's an enormous room and there's a fantastic view of the distant hills. The view must be wonderful from upstairs.'

'By the way,' he said, 'did Ella show you where we are to eat our meals—after tonight, that is?'

Paula's eyes widened. 'Do you mean we're to eat here—not with them?'

'The arrangement which the Richters seem to think will suit guests best is for them to eat here in private, which in turn leaves them free to enjoy their holiday,' Karl explained.

This was getting worse, Paula found herself thinking. What was this turning out to be—an opportunity to brood on a background to her proposed book, or a fake honeymoon?

As Karl showed her the dining-room, which was a mass of sun-filter curtaining, he said, 'Max was saying this used to be a solarium at one time. A room built mainly of glass to give exposure to the sun seems totally ridiculous in this part of the world, don't you think?'

Paula's eyes went from the four round dining-tables to the large dresser and sideboard. One of the tables was set for three.

'Normally, Karl, this would be a good idea — that is, when it comes to a family group or a group of close friends. . .'

'Or honeymooners,' he cut in. 'Is that what you are thinking?' There was more than a hint of angry sarcasm in his voice.

'Now that you mention it — yes.' Her voice was cool.

He went on looking at her for a moment, then he said, 'Across the corridor there is guest lounge.'

Paula began to leave the room. 'Karl, the Richters will be waiting. We're late enough as it is.'

Both Ella and Max were interested to hear that Paula was an architect, and during drinks which they had on the long veranda of the main house the conversation, polite and a trifle strained to begin with, revolved around the old house, which could be seen from where they were seated.

Paula was doing her best to appear interested,

but her mind was busy with how she had behaved with Karl at the abandoned house in the desert earlier that day. She was also aware that although he appeared to be interested in what Max was saying, Karl was thinking the same thing. Several times, in the lantern light, their eyes met and held in a long, explorative look.

How was it, she asked herself, that her life had suddenly begun to revolve around a castle commanding a view of a lonely coastline strewn with fragments of agate, a derelict house in the desert, and finally an old guest-house which rose incongruously from a boulder-strewn area on the edge of the desert? Although a pink Bavarian *schloss* was at the back of everything, it was extremely doubtful whether the playboy Count Karl von Buren would ever make her his wife and that she would, as a result, share this *schloss* with him.

As much as she was in love with Karl, she was finding it difficult to trust him, as more and more destructive evidence piled up in her mind against him.

'As you must have decided for yourselves, it was constructed in a most absurd and extravagant way,' Max was saying. 'When I bought the land, with the old house on it, it was absolutely dilapidated, but with its history, it seemed a pity to pull it down, and yet we ourselves did not wish to live in it. It was Heinrich, actually, who suggested a guest-house. We've known Heinrich for years. No doubt he has filled you in with the details of the love story which played itself out here and which can only be regarded as a disaster?'

Paula was puzzled, and yet something seemed to be taking her heart suddenly, and had begun to squeeze it. 'No, he hasn't, actually.'

'And so—you mean you don't know?' Max shook his head and turned to Ella. 'Isn't that just typical of the old boy?'

'Obviously he intended that Paula should find out for herself,' Ella replied, 'but yes, it is typical of Heinrich, I must admit.'

'Paula,' Max gave his attention to Paula again, 'the style of this old house is of the mode of house in Germany—mainly during 1912, although this house was built before that. Obviously,' he chuckled, 'this architect was ahead of his time. According to records on hand, some local material was used, but most of it was imported from Germany. In fact, one can hardly credit this, but the floors and walls were actually constructed in Germany and shipped over here—and then followed the big haul, by ox-wagons—and this is where Rory Stewart entered into the picture.'

'My great-grandfather—Rory Paul?' Paula drew a long breath. 'I—I—I'm completely staggered!'

'His grave is on the property,' Max told her. 'You will see it in the morning. You will have passed the small cemetery on the way here.'

Paula's thoughts immediately flew to the awareness she had felt as she and Karl had driven past the small, fenced-in area.

'You know, I've come to the conclusion that everybody seemed to have kept a record of events in this country,' Max continued, 'and the man who built the old house, as we always refer to it, was no exception. He was a man who was involved in illicit diamond dealings. Your great-grandfather, who by this time had acquired his own pouch of illicit diamonds, was tipped off about him and, together with a girl he'd met in Kolmanskop—she used to entertain in the casino there from time to time, I believe—the usual high-kicking good-time girl—he hitched a lift on one of the wagons which hauled building materials here, as I have explained. There were four of them—your great-grandfather, this girl, Olga, the owner of the ox-wagon and his *tou-leier*. You know, each ox had its own name and its own place, and from time to time, the *tou-leier* would get off the wagon to lead all the animals by calling out to them, often brandishing his whip but not always intending to hurt.'

As she listened Paula was endeavouring to control her natural reaction, which was to shed tears. Glancing at Karl, she said, 'Did you know about this—incredible story? Did Heinrich tell you?'

'No. I am as amazed as you are. Heinrich *did* mention, though, that you would possibly find material here to make your book possible.' Karl gave her a long look. 'No, Paula, I definitely did not know.'

Paula took a sip of her drink and saw her hand shaking. 'What happened?' she asked, looking at Max.

'Well, they reached here and they camped here, while the crafty negotiations concerning the illicit diamonds were taking place. What was going on, though, was that Olga was becoming involved with the man who had brought them this far in the wagon, and it was she who gave the whole game away. The owner of the wagon then bribed his *tou-leier* to beat up Rory Stewart one night, strip him of the pouch containing the diamonds—of which he was to have received his cut—and the three of them would then disappear into the night. The long and short of it, of course, was that the *tou-leier* was given the slip and the girl Olga and her new fancy-man made off with the diamonds, leaving him behind. The *tou-leier* also disappeared—from sheer fright. How far he got on foot is another matter.'

'Oh, don't tell me Rory was—*murdered*!' Paula took a long, shuddering breath. 'I—couldn't stand it!'

'No, Paula,' Ella broke into the story. 'Apparently he was badly beaten, but he recovered. His health was never the same, though. A friendship sprang to life between the owner of this place and your great-grandfather, who ended up working here, until he died while still a relatively young man. We'll take you to see his grave tomorrow.'

At this stage Max took over again. 'On Rory's deathbed, as the saying goes, he arranged — and paid — for the tombstone and the engraving on the stone.'

'This is an incredible story,' said Karl. 'A twist of fate if ever there was one!'

Sensing how tense Paula was, Max glanced at Karl. 'Heinrich tells me you have a pilot's licence?'

Karl picked up his glass. 'Yes, I do.'

At the back of her confusion Paula was thinking — another side to Karl. She imagined him at the controls of an aircraft — the handsome and dashing count.

'We thought you might enjoy to fly with us to the Welwitschia Plains,' said Max. 'We have a permit for this — that is, if you can bear to trust another pilot?'

'But of course,' laughed Karl. 'I'm not a botanist, but I'll be more than just a little interested to see these strange plants. I am sure I can speak for Paula.' Across the table, his grey and concerned eyes sought hers.

'Yes, I — look forward to it,' she agreed.

'Well, let's put it this way, you won't find these plants anywhere else in the world,' said Max. 'They have survived in one of the most desolate areas of the world for millions of years. The Welwitschia is virtually a living fossil. In years gone by they were seen only by those people with courage enough to travel over such greatly feared desert regions by ox-wagon and even on foot.'

Dinner was served in the ranch-like dining-room, where conversation was mainly about the small plane which the Richters owned.

The generator, it was explained to Paula and Karl, would go off at ten forty-five, but they would find lamps, candles and matches in their rooms.

As they walked back to the old house, Paula found herself shivering. 'The house looks haunted,' she said.

'Oh, nonsense!' Karl laughed a little. 'Surely you don't believe that?'

'I do,' she said. 'It looks spooky. From an architectural point of view the style is completely out of context with the surroundings. I mean — the corrugated-iron mansard roof. . .! It must be boiling under there. The mansard roof is perfect for snowy conditions, when the snow just slides off it, but it's not likely to snow here.'

'Look, would you like to change rooms with me?' Karl asked when they had entered the house. 'Maybe the idea of having two beds in your room is daunting to you? There is only one large bed in my room, which probably looks more personal.'

'No, Karl. Thank you all the same.' She placed her hands on her elbows and hugged herself.

'Let's not beat about the bush, Paula. Would you

like me to sleep in your room? After all, there are two beds — and we are not exactly strangers.'

'No, really.' Paula was beginning to feel impatient and restless. 'In the first place, Ella was saying that there's a small kitchen here, which is used by the maid who'll prepare our morning coffee and croissants. What would she think when she brings the coffee?'

'We don't have to think in terms of what the maid will think, surely?' he snapped. 'By the way, I've brought a bottle of sherry along. It's too soon to turn in after that large meal, don't you think?'

Paula's nerves were on edge, but she said, 'That will be nice. Where will we have it? In the guest lounge?'

'There is nothing more depressing than a visitor's lounge, especially since there happens to be two comfortable chairs and attractive lamps in both bedrooms.' He gave her a faint smile.

'What you're saying, Karl, is — whose room? Yours or mine? Is that it?'

'Look, in view of what has taken place here since we arrived, I realise, Paula, that you are tense. I am merely suggesting that we enjoy a nightcap together before going to bed after a heavy meal of roast lamb and vegetables, followed by an elaborate sweet concoction, but. . .' he lifted his shoulders impatiently, 'please yourself. What exactly is bothering you, though? Suppose you get to the point?'

'Well, yes, I'll do that, Karl. Hilda *was* your

fiancée, wasn't she? Why didn't you tell me? Why weren't you straight with me? When all is said and done, you'll probably go back to Germany and patch things up with her again. Herr Heinrich knew all the time — just as he seems to have known everything else.'

Karl was angry now. 'A lot of people, Paula, attach their own interpretation to a situation. Hilda and I were never engaged. I have already explained the position to you. Why do you go on with this? Once you begin, there is no stopping you. You exhaust everyone, including yourself.'

He left her to go and open his door and then, turning to look at her, he said, 'I will bring you a glass of sherry. It will help you to sleep — and by the way, there are better ways to amuse oneself than trying to make it with a reluctant and suspicious woman. You will be quite safe.'

Still smarting from his remark, Paula went into her room, but left the door open for him and when he arrived a moment or two later he was carrying two small glasses of sherry.

Taking one from him, she said stiffly, 'Thank you.' Her voice was soft and huffy. She watched him as he sat down and then leant back in his chair to look at her.

'I didn't know about your great-grandfather. You do believe that, don't you? It would have been better if you had been prepared for this news.'

'Yes, I suppose so,' she answered. 'Even though

all this took place so many years ago, it came as a shock, after all. I hated to think of him being beaten up. Judging by photographs of him back in Ireland, he was so handsome. He had a well-trimmed beard and moustache and his hair was curly and touched his neck, near to his collar. It—and the beard, of course—was a dark auburn. His eyes, according to my great-grandmother's diaries, were a startling blue.'

They were silent for a few moments, then Karl said quietly, 'You know, I was hoping that something more than researching a background to your book prompted you to leave with me this morning.'

'Actually, something did. I *wanted* to be with you.' Her eyes met his. As she put her glass down on the table her eyes followed him as he went back to his room to pour himself another sherry.

When he came back he said, 'You wanted to be with me, you say, and yet what it really amounts to is that when it comes to our relationship you are something like those shifting sands out there. You're here one moment and gone the next.'

'You could have been honest with me, Karl, about Hilda. Everybody seems to know that she was—and maybe still is—your fiancée.'

'That is so. I agree with you. Everybody seems to know—except *me!*' He was angry now. 'I have told you that she and I were not engaged. It's up to you, Paula. You have too many opinions about me—and all of them detrimental. Believe it or not, you are the only woman I have asked to be my wife. Goodnight. If you are nervous in the night, call me. I'll leave my door open.'

Apart from waking up once, when she had that eerie feeling that someone was there, Paula slept well after getting out of bed to open her door. In the filtering light she saw that Karl's door was open and she felt a strong impulse to go to him, but went back to her bed. Next time she awoke it was morning.

CHAPTER NINE

WEARING big sunglasses, Paula sat beside Karl in the Land Rover and made notes for her book. They had been exploring part of the largest nature reserve in Namibia which lay between the diamond Sperrgebiet in the south and the Swakop River in the north.

Apart from being driven round by Max Richter and shown the small cemetery where Rory Paul Stewart had been buried all those years ago, the past three days had been spent in much the same way.

Glancing at Karl, she found herself wondering why it was that women were so suspicious. Why were they so difficult when it came to forgiving a man? So jealous? Had Rory been so aware of this fact that he could not bring himself to go back home?

Karl broke into her thoughts. 'Would it not be more simple if you told me what is worrying you?'

For a moment she hesitated and then she decided to tell him. 'At the back of my mind, Karl, I keep wondering whether I'm to be discarded like Hilda.'

'So we are back to Hilda? Will you forget about

Hilda and those Alpine slopes? I'm sorry I ever mentioned that to you. I am more concerned with the present — and so should you be!'

They drove back in silence to the guest-house where Karl immediately poured them each a long, cold drink which they took along to the lounge from where they could sit and watch the sunset.

'Let's clear this up, Paula. I want you to forget about Hilda once and for all. It's over with her. It was that way before she decided to try again and came out to Namibia uninvited. You know, I've been thinking. To celebrate the completion of the restoration of Sturmvögel, let's visit the Etosha National Park I have heard so much about. After all, I am sure you will want to bring wild animals into your book, no?'

The tension which had been building up in Paula during the day increased, but, trying not to show it, she said, 'I suppose I might as well sling in a safari or two.'

'Well,' he sounded impatient, 'according to my research on this subject, we should be able to view vast herds of springbok, gemsbok, giraffe — not to mention lions — or do they say *lion*? We'll see elephants, black rhino and birds of all description.'

Her thoughts had become brooding and depressed as Karl was speaking. Max Richter had taken them to see Rory's grave, and as she had looked down at it she could hardly believe that this was the resting place of her great-grandfather.

What was more, was he really *resting*? Had he ever found peace?

'Paula?' Karl's voice was curt.

'Huh?' She gave him a blank stare. 'I'm sorry.'

'Forget it!' He turned away.

'No, don't be like that, Karl!' she pleaded.

'How do you expect me to be? I want us to do things together. Is that so unusual?'

'No.' She drew an impatient breath. '*I* want us to do things together. . .'

'In that case, what is the problem?'

'The problem is that I've learned a thing or two about you, Karl. When it comes to turning a situation to your own advantage, you're very experienced.'

'It appears that there is yet another game to play.' His voice had a hard, angry edge to it and his grey eyes were beginning to blaze. 'We are getting back to bath night, of course, no? And Hilda; not to mention the Alpine slopes. These things have become an obsession with you.'

'This isn't a game with me, Karl. I'm genuinely worried. I mean—OK, forget about Hilda and the slopes, but to get back to that night. It keeps cropping up in my mind, and I find it difficult to forget—and forgive, for that matter.'

She watched him as he whistled lightly between his teeth before he raked his dark hair back with his fingers.

'Believe me, I can understand that. I have apologised for this, and what is more, I meant it, but your mind keeps painting bad pictures of me—just as your great-grandfather Rory must have known that his wife would have done the same thing if he had gone back and it had got to her ears that he'd had an affair in Africa.'

'That's right, blame my great-grandmother for the fact that he didn't go back to Ireland!' Paula flung back at him.

'Why is it, Paula, that our relationship swivels from love and affection to hostility? Is it because it actually means so little to you?' asked Karl.

'It's because it means so much to me, actually. So much, in fact, that I keep asking myself questions.'

He put his glass down, then stood up and came over to her and reached for her hand. 'Come.' His voice was soft. 'If it means so much to you, why don't you prove it by trusting me?'

'How, Karl? By going to bed with you?'

'Yes. If you can trust yourself to trust me, why not? I have asked you to marry me, after all.'

'Yes, you have.' Her voice was soft.

'We will be married at Sturmvögel and we will be married again in the chapel back home. Apart from the masses of fresh flowers in the chapel and in the banqueting hall, there will be one desert rose on the bridal table. Do you see how romantic I am when it comes to you?' He stroked her hair. 'After the honeymoon, which definitely will not be held

anywhere near the Alpine slopes, we will live
happily ever after in a pink Bavarian *schloss*. Tell
me you love me, Paula. . .'

'I *do* love you, but please don't assume that I'm
going to end up in bed with you in this guest-house,
because I'm not. I don't have to prove I'm in love
with you by doing that.' She drew away from him.
'Do you realise, Karl, that it's nearly time to change
for dinner?'

'I'm watching the time.' His voice had grown
hard again.

They were flying to the Welwitschia Plains in the
morning, and Max had suggested that they all dine
together at the main house.

During dinner, Karl's moody eyes watched Paula
thoughtfully. Later, when they were back in the
guest-house, she told him she had a headache.

'In other words, you wish to be alone,' he said.
'Well, it's not a problem. Take a couple of headache
pills and go to bed. I hope you'll feel better in the
morning. Do you have anything for a headache? If
not, I have something.'

'I have something, thank you. It was probably
the sun today,' she told him.

'Probably.' His tone was curt and she knew he
did not believe her.

Taking off in the four-seater plane the following
morning was a thrilling experience. Max flew low
over the small cemetery, and Paula's thoughts

went to the kindness and understanding which Karl had shown her as she had gazed down at the grave the day before. Sensing her need to be alone when she had got down on her knees, he had indicated to Max that they should wander towards the gate and then they had gone to stand beside the Land Rover, talking quietly.

Her eyes had brimmed with tears as she had read the words which were engraved on the stone: 'But whoso committeth adultery with a woman lacketh understanding: he that doth it destroyeth his own soul.'

'You poor tormented soul,' she had whispered. 'Why don't you rest now, Rory? Rest now that you know somebody knows what happened all those years ago. In fact, I'm going to arrange to have this stone changed. I'll have the words "At Peace" engraved on it. I like to think you know I'm here.' Then she had placed a spray of the tough Hoodia Gordonii, known as the Queen of the Namib, above the name 'Rory Paul Stewart'. She had got out of the Land Rover to pick this spray on the way to the cemetery, and although the stems of the plant were armoured with spikes, the flowers resembled large dusky-pink morning glories.

Directly she had joined Karl and Max, Karl had taken her into his arms. 'He'll be at peace now, Paula. . .now that his story is known to a member of the family—his great-granddaughter. He is no different from anybody else—we all err and stray like lost sheep, no? Unfortunately, he strayed too far from home, and to him there was no going back.'

A short time later, Paula gazed down at the herds of gemsbok, springbok and mountain zebra and felt at peace herself. She felt happy to be with Karl.

Sensing her thoughts, Karl turned to look at her. 'You're beautiful,' he said softly. 'I love you.'

'I love you too,' she told him, and meant it.

From the air, it could be seen that the Welwitschias were inclined to grow along shallow watercourses which were formed by occasional rainstorms, but since rain in the area was negligible, the plants were undoubtedly kept alive by the frequent fogs which were carried from the coast across the dunes and gravel plains. This moisture was absorbed by the leaves and it collected there before trickling down to the soil below.

Max took the plane down on the dusty, hard-packed desert-sand alongside the scattered plants and a wood-framed sun shelter in which Ella lost no time in setting out the refreshments which had been brought along. Low, barren hills encircled the area.

As she studied one of the largest plants, Paula could hardly believe that it could be well over five thousand years old. On most plants there were only two broad leaves, but because of splitting, they gave the appearance of having a number of leaves.

As their guide, Max was obviously enjoying himself as he shared his knowledge of the famous plant with Paula and Karl.

Although she was interested, Paula was incredibly aware of Karl as they bent over the various plants together. She got satisfaction just from hearing him breathing softly, from feeling that breath against her cheek, from the touch of his warm arm against hers. When we get back to the old house, I *want* him to make love to me, she thought.

'It's interesting to note,' Max was saying cheerfully, 'that the female cones only, not the male cones, are home to these bugs. You can see how they suck the juice with their long tubular beaks. Do you see that, Paula?'

'Yes,' she answered quickly, and trying to sound intelligent. 'It's amazing!'

Feeling Karl's amused grey eyes on her, she glanced secretly at him and nearly laughed as he winked slyly in Max's direction.

As they walked about together a moment later, he said, 'I don't want to look at bugs. I only have eyes for you. Thank goodness *I* am not seven hundred years old, which appears to be the age of a moderate-sized Welwitschia plant — because then I would be too old to make love to you.'

Except for turbulence, which at one stage alarmed Paula but seemed to amuse Karl, the flight back to the stud farm was uneventful except for the fact that Ella brought up Hilda's name.

'What a pity your fiancée didn't come, after all. She would have loved all this, I'm sure!'

When Karl made no reply, Paula felt her mood beginning to change. Although she felt niggled by this and while depression was beginning to have its way with her, she tried not to show it.

As she and Karl dined together in the old house she was quiet, and eventually he said, 'You're very quiet, Paula. Don't tell me it's the sun again?' His tone was slightly mocking, but his eyes were thoughtful.

Trying to laugh a little, she said, 'What's it like to be a count, Karl?'

He laughed. 'Is that what you have been thinking about? All this time, while I have been thinking of making love to you?'

'Yes—also about my book, of course. Anyway, what's it like? You haven't answered my question.'

He shrugged his shoulders. 'Oh, it affords— advantages.'

The maid came to ask if there was anything else they would like and then left the house soon afterwards.

'You know, it has just struck me,' Karl was saying, 'that I brought a battery-operated tape deck along and completely forget about it. It's in the Land Rover—I'll go and get it. I think a little soft background music is in order while we enjoy a very good liqueur. Don't run away.' He came over to her and kissed her lightly on the forehead.

While she waited for him to get back from the Land Rover, Paula went to her room and stood at the huge windows gazing at the night shadows on the ground and the outline of the distant, barren hills. Her thoughts brooded on the fact that once again Karl had not explained the position about Hilda to Ella.

A moment later Karl tapped lightly on her door. 'Well, are you ready for that liqueur?'

She turned and, wanting to hurt him as he had hurt her, said, 'In other words, come into my parlour, said the spider to the fly?'

There was an immediate gleam of anger in his eyes.

'I have hardly had time to spin a web. Besides, since when have you become my prey—just as Rory Stewart became the prey of a girl named Olga and her ox-wagon driver? Paula, to get back to what is always on your mind—no man in his right senses would have done what I did to you that night at Sturmvögel. *I* wasn't in my right senses— so why the hell can't we forget it?'

In an effort to recapture the way she had felt about him in the plane and at the Welwitschia Plains she said, 'I was *joking*, Karl.'

'Well, would it be asking too much to suggest that you joke about something else?'

'Not at all.' Her voice was frigid.

A few moments later she sat on one of the big chairs in his room and stared moodily at him, while he filled the small glasses he had brought along from Sturmvögel.

'Is this tape to your liking,' he asked curtly, 'or would you prefer something else?'

'It's very romantic. Just right.' His abrupt tone had succeeded in annoying her. 'But isn't that what you'd intended?'

'What would you have preferred?' he snapped. 'Italian opera?'

'I'm not complaining. It's a very nice tape, actually.'

'Good,' he said shortly.

They sat in silence for a while, then Paula broke it. 'Don't sulk, Karl. I told you I was joking!'

'It's the other way around. *You* are the one who sulks and suffers from mood swings, lady.'

There was a stunned silence before Paula stood up. 'I think I'll have my liqueur in my room, so I'll say goodnight.'

Their eyes met and clung together like taut wire. The expression on Karl's face was hard. 'Don't go, said the spider to the fly. I have an attractive shower cubicle in my bathroom. Maybe we should put it to good use?'

Paul felt suddenly threatened by his mood.

'Although I do not have eight legs like a spider,' he went on, 'I hope, even at this stage, to begin to spin a web. Isn't that expected of me, after all?'

'Oh, Karl, this is ridiculous! I've brought a very good book along — so I'll say goodnight.'

'A good book, huh? Since we arrived here, Paula, you have been playing one of the oldest games in the book, do you know that? In case you don't, it's called stalling.'

'And *you* haven't been playing games, of course?' Her voice was bitter. 'Why is it, for instance, that you've never bothered to correct Ella when she refers to Hilda as your fiancée?'

'I see no reason to discuss Hilda. As for games, why should I play games? Why should I waste my time? I am honest enough to confess that my life has changed since I met you.'

'In that case, you have my sympathy. Change is rarely easy, after all—especially a drastic one. Oh, *Karl*, I don't think you realise—this is a very intense situation for me. On the one hand I want us to make love, and on the other I'm a cautious person. Quite apart from that, I can almost see my great-grandfather's grave from here. Don't you see?'

'No, I don't see. What happened to your great-grandfather happened a long time ago. You speak about being a cautious person. You don't have to be cautious with me. . .'

'Call me a prude, then,' she cut in. 'I'm a prude!'

'One who affects excessive modesty, in other words?'

'My modesty is very real,' Paula assured him.

'Is that why you are here in my room—because your modesty is very real?'

The question was true enough to humiliate her. 'That's unfair, and you know it! You know why I'm here. You know, I can't believe you said that, Karl.'

His face was cold now. 'It was my turn to joke. Anyway, if nothing else, I can see you to your door.'

'I'll see myself to my door, thank you. I can't believe we've ended up this way. We've had such a wonderful day. What went wrong?' Her troubled eyes searched his.

'Ask yourself that question, Paula.' He turned away from her and went to stand at the large window.

Later, in bed, the book which she had brought along held little interest as she fumed and fretted. She was still awake when the generator dimmed the lights twice in warning that it would go off shortly, thus allowing time for lamps and candles to be lit, if necessary.

Eventually she slept, but her slumber was restless and punctuated by dreams of desert, boulders and bare hills in which she appeared lost as she ran barefoot. Directly she woke up she went cold and reached for the torch she had brought along. Its beam revealed nothing, and yet she had been distinctly aware of an eerie presence.

After lighting a lamp, she got up to open the door — and caught her breath as she saw a figure in the corridor, then Karl said, 'I thought I heard you call out!'

'I had a nightmare,' she told him. 'It was rather awful and woke me up, and then I distinctly felt his presence. I've felt it before.'

Coming over to her, Karl said, 'Oh, come, you're letting your imagination get the better of you.' His voice was impatient. 'He's at peace now.'

'No, I'm not letting my imagination get the better of me! I *know* what I felt, Karl. Maybe he came to tell me.'

Karl closed the distance between them and she could almost feel the warmth of his body through her satin nightshirt, and her eyes went over his bare torso, for he was wearing nothing but a pair of shorts.

'Your teeth are chattering,' he said. 'If you are so nervous, change rooms with me.'

'Karl, I could have wept with disappointment when you let me go tonight,' she whispered.

His expression didn't change, and he continued to watch her. 'So?'

'So — I want to be with you.'

'If this is the effect a nightmare produces, then the nightmare was worthwhile, no?' He took her into his arms, then held her closer, as though as an indication of his protection. Then he lifted her up and carried her to his room, pushing the door closed with his shoulder, before moving towards the big bed.

She allowed him to slip the nightshirt over her shoulders before he shrugged himself out of his shorts. A moment later she felt his delicious nakedness against her own.

'Forget the past,' he told her. 'I love you.'

'I love you too. I *do*, Karl.'

Vaguely she was aware that the bedlinen carried the scent of him—extra-good soap, the lingering fragrance of his aftershave lotion and even the sunny scent of his skin.

She had the feeling that her breasts were tight buds, and as he kissed them they began to ripen and blossom, not only for her own pleasure, but for his.

In turn, she kissed and teased his nipples with the tip of her tongue, and their lips met hungrily. Karl's hands went to her head and he buried his fingers in her hair as he pressed her face against his own.

Behind closed eyes she could almost see his hands as they caressed and became familiar with her body. He was, she thought, awakening in her sensations she never realised existed. It was the first time that she had been completely alive, and she felt an almost frantic excitement.

Shyly at first, she began to explore his body, and as he finally took possession of her eager body she was aware of a thrust of primitive pleasure before being carried along by him.

It was something like the sandstorm they had

seen together from inside the derelict house, when the wind-heaped mass of sand was carried along until it had gathered full force and then spent itself.

Afterwards, her hair felt damp and so did his, but she snuggled into him, seeking the warmth, affection and love which he had to give her.

By the time they awoke the sky was aflame and there was the aroma of coffee and the muffled clinking of coffee-cups coming from the small kitchen.

Paula gasped, then sat up. 'Oh—the maid! Is that the time already?'

In almost one movement Karl was out of bed, and as he dressed he said, 'I'll go and collect the trays from her.'

'Prude!' Paula mocked. 'You're a prude, Karl!'

'One who affects excessive modesty, in other words?' He laughed. 'But, like yours, my modesty is very real.'

'Ha, ha,' she mocked.

He came over and kissed her quickly. 'Your eyes are long and lazy. Now I wonder why that is?'

'Maybe, for some unknown reason, they're just changing shape.' She smiled up at him.

'You know the reason,' he said, 'and so do I.'

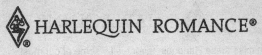

HARLEQUIN ROMANCE®

brings you

Stories that celebrate love, families and children!

Watch for our second Kids & Kisses title in *July*.

Island Child
by Roz Denny
Harlequin Romance #3320

Full of warmth, love and laughter. A story about what family *really means, by the author of* Romantic Notions *and* Stubborn as a Mule.

> Sarah Michaels is a single mother with an eight-year-old son. She knows that a boy needs a male role model, a man to look up to and have fun with. That's why she signed up with Befriend an Island Child.
>
> The agency sends Gabe Parker. Her son, Mike, is immediately crazy about him. But Sarah...well, Sarah's not so sure. The problem is, he reminds her of her ex-husband—in all the wrong ways.

Available wherever Harlequin books are sold.

HARLEQUIN®

Don't miss these Harlequin favorites by some of our most
distinguished authors!
And now, you can receive a discount by ordering two or more titles!

HT #25551	THE OTHER WOMAN by Candace Schuler	$2.99	☐
HT #25539	FOOLS RUSH IN by Vicki Lewis Thompson	$2.99	☐
HP #11550	THE GOLDEN GREEK by Sally Wentworth	$2.89	☐
HP #11603	PAST ALL REASON by Kay Thorpe	$2.99	☐
HR #03228	MEANT FOR EACH OTHER by Rebecca Winters	$2.89	☐
HR #03268	THE BAD PENNY by Susan Fox	$2.99	☐
HS #70532	TOUCH THE DAWN by Karen Young	$3.39	☐
HS #70540	FOR THE LOVE OF IVY by Barbara Kaye	$3.39	☐
HI #22177	MINDGAME by Laura Pender	$2.79	☐
HI #22214	TO DIE FOR by M.J. Rodgers	$2.89	☐
HAR #16421	HAPPY NEW YEAR, DARLING by Margaret St. George	$3.29	☐
HAR #16507	THE UNEXPECTED GROOM by Muriel Jensen	$3.50	☐
HH #28774	SPINDRIFT by Miranda Jarrett	$3.99	☐
HH #28782	SWEET SENSATIONS by Julie Tetel	$3.99	☐

Harlequin Promotional Titles

#83259	UNTAMED MAVERICK HEARTS (Short-story collection featuring Heather Graham Pozzessere, Patricia Potter, Joan Johnston)	$4.99	☐

(limited quantities available on certain titles)

	AMOUNT	$
DEDUCT:	10% DISCOUNT FOR 2+ BOOKS	$
	POSTAGE & HANDLING	$
	($1.00 for one book, 50¢ for each additional)	
	APPLICABLE TAXES*	$ _____
	TOTAL PAYABLE	$ _____
	(check or money order—please do not send cash)	

To order, complete this form and send it, along with a check or money order for the
total above, payable to Harlequin Books, to: **In the U.S.:** 3010 Walden Avenue,
P.O. Box 9047, Buffalo, NY 14269-9047; **In Canada:** P.O. Box 613, Fort Erie, Ontario,
L2A 5X3.

Name: _____

Address: _____ City: _____

State/Prov.: _____ Zip/Postal Code: _____

*New York residents remit applicable sales taxes.
 Canadian residents remit applicable GST and provincial taxes.

HBACK-AJ